Heartland Humor

It's Hard to Push a Lawnmower Through the Snow

Don Gadow

Published by Treasurabilia Publishing

Copyright © Treasurabilia Publishing 1992, 2019, 2023

ISBN 978-0-9639135-6-2

This book is to be regarded as a work of fiction. Though many stories are taken from the author's life, character names are fictional, and the characters and personalities are meant to reflect general human traits rather than any specific person.

With the exception of "Garge sales, "The law of the corn," and "Big shedders," the following stories were first published in slightly different form in the Annandale *Advocate* between 1983 and 1990 and are reprinted with permission.

Contents

Chapter 1

Interview with myself

Those who heard my appearance on KMOM-Monticello radio must have been disappointed. Because this interview was limited to two minutes instead of the hour I deserved, the announcer didn't have time to plumb my complex psyche. Nor did he ask the right questions that would have brought out the spontaneous humor I had carefully pre-planned. In order to get the truth on record, I have rewritten the interview – the way it should have happened.

Q. We are interviewing Don Gadow of Annandale, a free-lance writer and leading spokesman for the feminist movement. Don, what is a free-lance writer?

A. Well, you got a few things wrong there. First of all, when I talked to you last week, I said I was a leading connoisseur of femininity. Also, as a free-lance writer I'm a diplomat without portfolio.

Q. What do you mean?

A. Aside from my *Advocate* columns and articles, I have only a couple of pieces published. My articles are too cerebral for magazines like *Harpers, Redbook,* or *Playboy*; for magazines that pay a good price for a quality article or story.

Q. Then how do you define a free-lance writer?

A. A free-lance writer tries to make a living from his writing. He has a nose for news. He's the kind of person who runs over a porcupine on the way to the lake cabin, goes home and checks six porcupine books out of the library, and sells an article on "our spiny friends" to the *Reader's Digest* for $5,000. He tells us more than we ever can imagine about a topic we could care less about.

Q. Then how do you describe yourself?

A. The free-lance writer writes on something he doesn't care about to make a dollar. I write on things nobody cares about, and I don't make a living.

Q. Why not follow the free-lance path?

A. And give up my principles? "Broke but Happy," that's my song.

Q. Who are some of the main influences on your writing?

A. Mostly humorists and satirists. Russell Baker, Art Buchwald, Andy Rooney, Mark Russel (but not when he sings on those TV specials), Mark Twain, Rudyard Kipling, Erma Bombeck – say, she gets more mileage writing about panty hose than any woman ever did wearing them. Oh, and I read President Reagan's old speeches.

Q. You say you write an occasional column for the Annandale *Advocate*. What's an occasional column?

A. It's when I get around to it, when the fish don't bite, when I get snubbed in a bar, or when I have an extreme pain, say a kidney stone attack. Or when I read the *National Enquirer* in the barber shop.

Q. What's the name of your column?

A. It doesn't have a name yet. I haven't got around to that yet.

Q. How long have you been writing this column?

A. Five years.

Q. What subjects do you write about besides ice fishing cars? I read your recent column on that topic.

A. Important things. Nehru jackets, leisure suits, the polyester menace, excessive lawn mowing.

Q. Are there any topics you won't write about?

A. Religion, politics, and women's lib.

Q. Why those in particular?

A. I might be simple but I'm not crazy. I leave those topics for the experts.

Q. Describe you work methods. When do you do most of your writing?

A. Mornings between eight and nine. I don't want to burn myself out.

Q. Isn't that a rather short day?

A. Not for brain work. If all politicians concentrated for an hour a day, we wouldn't have the kind of mess we do now.

Q. Would you describe yourself as a fast writer or a slow writer?

A. A half slow writer.

Q. Has your life changed since you began writing your column?

A. Yes, fewer people talk to me now. I get comments like, "Don't put that in the paper." I go on a fishing trip with the guys, and somebody says, "Don't write up this trip." It seems to inhibit people, especially those with things to hide, like mistakes they make. I go up town, and people cross the street when they see me coming.

Q. Didn't they always do that?

A. No, they usually just ignored me.

Q. What awards has your column won?

A. One was from the National Newspaper Association. Recently the Suomi Anti-Defamation League honored me as one of the 10 most bigoted for my trenchant attack on Finnish fish head soup – the meal that watches you eat.

Q. How many fan letters do you receive?

A. Two or three.

Q. A day?

A. No, in five years.

Q. Do you ever get calls from people who don't like your articles?

A. Yes. For instance, one March I wrote a column about moving my lawn while the snow was still on the ground. Well, a guy called up, angry. He said, "Did you really mow your ###!&====@*# lawn already?" When I affirmed, he said, "You +++##$$ creep, %^%&#* creep, you #$%%^#*&*. How could you be so !!#$#$#@ stupid?" 'Just born that way," I said. My ear rang as he slammed the receiver down.

Q. What was his problem?

A. I mowed before he did.

Q. Did you really mow while there was still now on the ground?

A. Yes.

Q. How could you be so @##!!@*# stupid? Oops! Missed the kill button. Seriously, how do you get your ideas for your columns?

A. I listen to what people say, read tabloid papers and shoppers. For instance, I read a home economics column on using left overs. Then I try to think of other uses. For example, if the chili has been kept in the refrigerator too long, make your own penicillin from the mold. Need bread crumbs for meatballs? Turn the toaster upside down and shake it out. I like to think of myself as a kind of household engineer.

Q. Do you use any other techniques to fight writer's block?

A. If everything else fails, I open up the dictionary at random and poke my finger down on a word. Then I just sit at the typewriter and free associate. Let's say the word is "marriage." Somebody once said, "It's the only license you take out after the hunt is over." That's borrowed, so I can't use it. I try a few other variations: "A license to fight, argument by law." Then I try a monologue: "Hey, have I got a job for You! No transportation costs. You work in the same place 24 hours a day. The boss comes home every evening to give work orders. You get to eat all your meals in. You get your choice of food every day because you fix it yourself. There's no overtime pay, but you get to sleep on the job. Sounds like an offer you can't refuse."

Q. Say, that's some awfully offensive stuff. How can you write something like that in the paper?

A. I can't. It's just an example of free association.

Q. Well, it's time to get back to our T. Texas Tyler retrospective. I can see the switchboard is going wild. Must be lots of listeners out there calling to compliment us on this interview.

Chapter 2
Confessions of a wood junkie

I'm recovering now, and like most proselytes, I feel compelled to share this life-changing experience with others who may be suffering from the same addition that enslaved me for five years.

The first step to recovery is to realize you have a problem. If your lifestyle matches at least three of the following symptoms, you may be, as I once was, a wood junkie. You may already be over the edge if...

You worry that somebody else, somewhere, anywhere, has a bigger woodpile.

You have six cords of dried oak, but you cut and burn green elm to save the oak "for later."

You find yourself standing with other firewood groupies staring up at a tree in the first stages of Dutch Elm Disease.

You find yourself cutting up cottonwood and willow and saying, "It all burns."

Your favorite meal is steak, served with mushrooms picked from your woodpile.

You take the wife out for a Sunday drive, but only to estimate the cords of wood in strangers' yards.

Instead of taking your wife out for a Sunday drive or watching the new and improved Vikings, you go out to cut wood.

You follow the summer storms from town to town like a gypsy roofer, passing out cards: "Have chainsaw, will cut up."

Your neighbor plants a maple sapling. You hallucinate. It's four feet thick, he's dead, and you're cutting it down.

You come home after a hard night's card playing only to find that your wife has installed over the television a decoupage of "The Cost of a Cord of Wood:" "Chain saw $450, maul and wedges $25, four-wheel drive pickup $16,000, new rear pickup window $225, etc... ."

You sneak out of town at 6 a.m. so nobody will find out where you're cutting your wood.

You follow your neighbor out of town at 6 a.m. to find out where he's cutting his wood.

You attend a social function, but instead of flirting with the ladies you join the men for chainsaw talk.

You find yourself a frequent transgressor against the Decalogue, but instead of your neighbor's wife, you covet his woodpile.

If you now recognize yourself as a wood junkie in desperate need of help, don't despair. At no charge I will summarize the advice I obtained for $75 an hour from a Twin City hypnotist who has worked with many professional athletes as well as chain saw addicts:

Take time to smell the roses.

There is beauty in a living, standing tree.

A man is not measured by the size of his woodpile.

No one person can cut all the dead trees in Wright County.

How much wood does one man need?

If this philosophy doesn't bring you back to reality, keep in mind what the old timer told me at the cost of three boilermakers in the South Haven liquor store: "Neffer caht mower dan vun yearce vood ahad, cuss if yew die, den saamboddy elce vill gat da vood."

Chapter 3

What price glory - $300

My life is a checkerboard of honors, but never did I get more attention than the time my name was drawn for the $300 Annandale Chamber of Commerce Crazy Cash Sweepstakes – and I wasn't present to win.

These are just a few past achievements that have great significance to me…

Drumming with the Jolly Steiners Vail Township Band the year we won the county 4-H Share the Fun talent contest.

Being singled out by my high school band director as the only tuba player in the world who doesn't know the "Colonel Bogey March."

Wearing the most coveted uniform owned by the Wabasso amateur baseball team, the Schell's Deer Brand Beer shirt. "It's plenty big on you," the manager said when we had bases loaded. "Just lean over the plate and take one in the front where it bags out."

Victim of the Gordon shift – the Milroy Yankees brought the left fielder into the infield and dared me to pull the ball deep. (Due to the illegible handwriting of our manager, my name invariably appeared in the Redwood Gazette box scores as Don - sometimes Dan – Gordon.) I didn't.

Entering on a dare and winning the Mankato State homecoming slogan contest in 1959 with a motto borrowed from an obscene joke.

Appearing as guest singer with the Elmer Schimmelpfennig Concertina Band about midnight during their farewell appearance at the Valhalla Ballroom.

Hearing my name and biography read in Spanish over the radio in Pueblo,

Colorado. Later being called just about everything in Spanish but a "cool dude."

Spending 22 years as a high school English teacher without becoming institutionalized.

Winning third place in a Tim Conway look-alike contest at the Triangle Bar on the West Bank.

Being the favorite target at the dunking stand for three straight years during the Dakota County Fair.

Earning the nickname "Cal" as the Calvin Griffith of the Annandale Lakers baseball franchise.

Receiving an "A" for my "Wood Junkie" article in a mass communications class at St. Cloud State University even though I had never enrolled in the class.

As flattering as these honors are, they pale in comparison to not winning the Crazy Cash Sweepstakes. Several weeks later, people still stopped me on the street to mention my loss.

Just as people still talk about where they were when the Twins won the 1987 World Series, I suspect that years from now I will remember where I was when my name was drawn. I certainly wasn't standing on the main street of downtown Annandale. I was out in a cornfield exhorting detasslers to "be happy" in their work. I didn't hear the bad news until that evening at the Methodist chicken barbeque.

A few days later I received the consolation prize in the mail. In the meantime, hundreds of people commiserated with me. Hundreds more treated me with that peculiar attitude the Germans call *schadenfreude*, which translates as enjoyment of other people's misfortunes. The kind of people who are secretly glad when they hear you lost a big walleye because your line broke.

Friends were torn between sympathy and joy because the prize would be bigger at the next Saturday's drawing. I was the Sad Sack. The news spread rapidly among the summer lake residents, who approached me on the streets with the curiosity of a scientist examining an especially repulsive bug under a microscope.

Senior citizens treated me the best. They had experienced the Great Depression. As they approached me on the streets, heads shaking slowly from side to side, I knew what was coming. "Aren't you the young man who wasn't there to win the money uptown? Too bad." It was like saying to George Washington, "Aren't you the guy with the wooden teeth?"

Inspirational sayings helped some. To those who said, "If you would be in good repute, let not the sun find you in bed." I responded, "It shall be small care to the high and happy conscience, what jealous friends, or envious foes, or common fools may judge." When others suggested, "To well deserve is somewhat, in spite of ill success." I countered with, "A good name is to be chosen rather than great riches."

I tried defense mechanisms: "I would rather sell four cords of wood and earn money the American way rather than take something for nothing." No one took me seriously. "I still got some money," I said, "a gift certificate good at local merchants, but the prize is discounted some."

"Yeah, by $295," they would answer.

By the second week of recovery, I had become a folk hero. Gossip had elevated the lost cash to $450. Then $600. Such is the stuff by which sagas are made. Beowulf never had it so good.

I still have the 4-H pin, some yellowed baseball clippings, a college homecoming button, a teaching certificate, and the five-dollar Crazy Cash consolation prize. I still suffer from guilt, embarrassment, persecution, and loss. If you want to keep yourself on an even keel, you'd better remember the advice of the poet, John Milton, who said, "If you sign up for a *must be present* drawing, stand uptown every Saturday and wait until your name is called."

Chapter 4

Gas tank existentialism

At 155,000 miles my 1980 Plymouth Volare is the Herschel Walker of automobiles – strong pride but dead in the clutch. Out on the open highway when I come up behind a tractor pulling a manure spreader, I'm encouraged to pass by Ricardo Montalban, who sits beside me beaming assurances as he sings something in Italian. But in the background, I hear a soft voice cautioning, "Boss! Boss!"

Still, the gas mileage is pretty good on my weekly trips back and forth between Winona State University, where I work, and Annandale. A recent tankful carried me from Winona to Annandale, back to Winona, and halfway back between Minnieska and Kellogg. My eightysomething mother wouldn't walk for gas, so I sat tight, counting the eagles and waiting for a Good Samaritan.

It's a common sight to see pedestrians carrying gas cans along Highway 61, as familiar as barges running up and down the Mississippi. These people are not stupid, careless, or forgetful. They are true rugged individualists.

The person who runs out of gas reminds me of a Guindon cartoon that shows two workmen staring at a large carton, its "This Side Up" instructions upside down. One man says to the other, "I don't take orders from a carton."

Seeing how far we can go on a tank of gas is one of the few remaining ways we can assert our personhood. It's a way to show we are superior to the machine. It's a way to control our destiny in a time when almost every enjoyable human activity is hampered by timetables, work rules, diet charts, and moral and ethical restraints.

No federal or state regulations or local ordinances require us to buy gas before the engine coughs and dies. The person who watches to see how low the needle can sink before the car glides to a halt is the real existentialist pushing that boulder up the hill.

Even my conservative wife has picked up the habit. One week when the Volare was between its seventh and eighth lives I had to borrow her car for the Winona trip. I was curious to see how far the Tempo would go on a tank of gas, so I didn't fill up before leaving for the return trip to Annandale. I found out later she had to push the car the last 20 feet to the gas pump. At first, she was angry, but then I reminded her how luck y she was that she hadn't stalled 10 miles out of town. That would have been one long push.

We do the same thing with our taxes. While we can't resist the April 15 deadline without paying an awful penalty, we can put off filing until the last minute. "They didn't make interest off my tax bill," one visionary told me at 4 p.m. on Tax Day as we stood in line at the post office to pay obeisance to the IRS. "Let the mail pile up," he said. "They will get my 56 dollars, but they had to wait for it."

So, the next time you see someone toting a gas can along the highway, remember he's exploring his own Fantasy Island. Honk the horn and wave as you speed past.

Chapter 5

Winter survival skills

"These are the times that try men's batteries," my neighbor said last winter when he came over to jump start my car. "Why do we have to suffer through this again?" we ask year after year. "Do we deserve this retribution? Watching the state legislature in action is punishment enough, without winter too," we say. Still, we have to survive, and to cope with 50 below windchill, we can't be mere stoics who grin and bear it.

Unless we take a lesson from the typical college students, who grin and "bare" it. On the campus young people live by a twisted Minnesota machismo or machisma – no boots, no hats, no scarves, no gloves or mittens that cost less than 50 dollars a pair. They wear earmuffs only when attached to rap music. Crosswalks are for sissies; scholars find a snowbank to march through bare ankled. Classrooms take on the smell of a locker room, as dozens of pairs of tube socks fester into expensive athletic shoes.

The swinging bachelor makes his own adaption. Instead of hanging around in fern bars, he cruises parking lots looking for attractive young ladies in need of his booster cables. The more sedentary content ourselves with driving around counting the number of cars per block with hoods up, the way as kids we used to look for license plates from all the states. Of course, we can only take a census if our own cars start up, and how good we feel then!

Some people refuse to knuckle under to Mr. and Ms. Frost. They snowmobile, ice fish, ski, go to their jobs. Other dig in for the duration, content to watch *Leave it to Beaver*, eat chocolate, and read romance novels. Or drink beer and hope for romance. Cabin fever is no paper tiger for these people. Domestic strife is the norm, murder staved off only by the thin veneer of civilization separating us from the caves.

If you're one of these shut-ins, your mind is like a chimney that needs sweeping. You need a long list of common-sense indoor activities to carry you through the next blizzard or Arctic cold front. You need a plan.

You could replay your Slim Whitman records, stage a neighborhood Victor Mature film festival, figure out your odds of winning the Publisher's Clearing House 10-million-dollar prize, rescue Canterbury Downs. Make out new lists of excuses for home, work, and school. Help your kids with their school excuses.

Work out a solution to the farm problem. If this is too easy, move on to educational reform. Simplify state and federal tax forms, redesign Star Wars, balance your checkbook, file the cents off coupons, improve Governor Carlson's image.

Ponder the imponderables: Why doesn't fast food cheese melt? Who invented the window envelope? And why? What's fun about burpless cucumbers? Why don't restaurant thermos coffee servers keep coffee hot? Could I clean out the refrigerator? Where do the missing letters go after they flee the motel sign? Could they sell cars if the balloon had never been invented?

Think the unthinkable: Attain a complete mastery of written English. Learn how to use the word "parameters." Invite Rudy Perpich back to Minnesota and donate to his campaign for whatever. Reweb the lawn chairs. Require your kids to participate in a family spelling bee. Exorcise the relatives you don't like from your photograph album. Polish the bones of your family skeletons.

Take your life on new journeys: Take a simple topic and complicate it. Chart a new course for America. Join ACE – American Cynics on Edge. Pay homage to the parsnip – after all, while we're suffering from the cold, the parsnip is luxuriating in the garden. Clean out the garage so you can put your car in it the next time it gets cold. Invent a new fad, like how to use pasta besides eating it. Cut the bills in half by throwing away the unpaid, overdue duplicates. Learn to deal off the top of the deck. Just say maybe.

If you spend your winters south of Des Moines, you can ignore all these suggestions. You can help others instead. Next spring call up everyone you know and invite them over to see your slides of Mexico, display your tan, ask them how they survived the big freeze, and then run like heck.

Chapter 6

It's hard to push a lawn mower through the snow

Inspired by the false spring, I mowed my lawn. "You're as balmy as the weather," I was told, but I pushed onward. Sure, it was tough going because of the snow, but the pleasure of being the first person in town to mow made the effort worthwhile.

Each year I have strived to be the mowing leader. Each year fate conspires against me. One March, the mower wouldn't crank because it was too cold. One spring I had to work, and the neighbors on unemployment got ahead of me again. Another year I came home from ice fishing, feeling like a proud warrior, to hear a stereo network of power engines emanating from every corner of the neighborhood.

Now with the thatcher-mulcher, people hurry out early each spring to chop up leaf residue, dead grass, eggshells, pop cans, lumber cut-offs, and other trash that accumulates around a yard over winter.

When I was a kid I hated moving the lawn. Well, *lawn* doesn't really describe what we had behind the house. It was a half-acre of quack grass, dandelions, and purple loosestrife running amok, the chore spiced up by the residue from a flock of geese that would quickly dye your shoes six different colors.

In those days people prided themselves on rugged individualism. Emerson's self-reliance aphorisms hung on every boys' bedroom walls (I can't speak for what girls displayed on their walls). My family would never use an engine to do what could be done by hand. No, we (I) mowed with a muscle-powered reel mower, the kind that gently bends over the long stems of grass and weeds without inflicting mortal harm. Staring out at this backyard, I often wished I could swap the lawn mower for the manure fork of Hercules.

I wasn't very old before I realized that grass, once cut, will grow again. It wasn't like a school lesson, which once learned could be forgotten immediately after the test.

By the time my dad bought a power mower, I had lost all interest in mowing and spent as much time as possible downtown in the pool hall, where the color green was more attractive.

Years later my wife and I bought a small house in Lakeville, 15 convenient miles from Metropolitan Stadium. I certainly didn't intend to let lawn mowing interfere with Twins games. Besides, there were ecological reasons for leaving the yard bare: conservation of fossil fuels, the oxygen given off by tall weeds that I didn't have to plant and fertilize, the exercise I would gain in the fall raking out tumbleweeds.

About the middle of July a delegation of lawn police arrived at the door to ask when I was planning to put in the lawn. "It's lowering neighborhood property values. It's a blight on the town. It's un-American," they said. These were the Goldwater years.

I wasn't ignorant of the mowing competition on my block. The mowers started up before 8 a.m. on Saturdays, as though some guru of suburbia was chanting, "Gentlemen, start your engines." They mowed every Tuesday and Thursday also. They adjusted their mowers for the closest cut possible.

"I march to a different drummer," I told the group. I was always ahead of my time – this was five years before Haight-Asbury. "I don't even own a lawn mower," I told them.

"You better march out of town then. If you don't put in a lawn soon, we'll get the city council after you. You can forget the snowmobile club too."

I planted grass seed and bought a mower. Seeing the seed sprout and grow tall softened me, I guess. It was like watching a child growing up. Of course, the analogy is flawed. People don't watch their children grow up and then chop them shorter.

One day I cut the grass for the first time, tearing into the job enthusiastically, feeling good that this was my own lawn, my possession, my identity.

For the first time I was conscious of the esthetics of lawn mowing. The smell of the fresh cut dewy grass blended with gasoline fumes. My ears thrilled to the unmuffled Briggs and Stratton that powered my used ten-dollar machine. Green flecks plastered the pebble-grain of my Florsheim wingtips. Clouds of culices rose from the grass. Women came out of their houses to watch. My glasses steamed over with pleasure. When the job was finished, I shut off the mower and stared at my work. "It sure is short," I said proudly.

The enjoyment soon wore off, as I realized that grass had to be cut more than once a month. Since I was coaching debate and gone every Saturday for tournaments, my mowing got off schedule irreparably. I started mowing on Mondays, the only day of the week I didn't hold debate practice. Since my neighbors mowed on Saturdays, their lawns looked tacky a day sooner. That first Monday lawn mowers buzzed until midnight as people around town desperately tried to catch up. Once again, I was ostracized.

At this point I decided to move to Annandale, which looked to me like the kind of laid back community where people let their dogs and lawns run loose. I soon learned that lawn mowing was just as serious out in the country. As a teaching colleague said, "Lawnliness is next to Godliness."

In Arizona people pave over their lawns with green asphalt. That's a good idea. Homeowners save on irrigation water, gasoline, and exercise. Their kids can play street hockey in their yards all summer, and everyone can have a tennis court.

Chapter 7
Lake Wobegon: the movie

WCCO, "Real Radio," proclaimed another disaster. "All roads leading into the St. Paul and Minneapolis downtown areas are hopelessly jammed. Take alternate routes. I knew. I was already in the thick of it, sandwiched among thousands of Hondas and Volvos bedecked with bumper stickers advertising Powdermilk Biscuits, Raw Bits, and the Lake Wobegon Truckstop (eat and get gas here).

"Well, hello love," I exclaimed, with clenched teeth. I did what the rest were already doing. I abandoned my car on I-94 and started hoofing it to the Metrodome. There was no way in Stearns County I would miss the premier of Garrison Keillor's *Lake Wobegon Days: The Movie*, subtitled, "Stinky Cheese," the motto of his Norwegian bachelor farmers.

However, I wouldn't be seeing it from the refurbished World Theater in downtown St. Paul. Those 5,000 tickets sold out at a grand each to benefit the Minnesota Zoo's new aquatic mammal surgical hospital. No, my fate was to sit encased in the tomb-like blues of HHH Stadium with 50,000 other lucky ticket holders.

I was better off than most. My $55 had netted me a prime seat down the third base line in the 20th row, certainly a better view than was in store for those in the upper deck, where the movie would be replayed on the electronic scoreboard.

Just outside Gate H, I squeezed past a clutch of Grateful Deadheads who hadn't figured out that the Bob Dylan concert had ended a year before. "Go home," I said. "Your way of life is finished – it's over."

"Cool, man," responded a lady in beaded buckskin, snakeskin head band,

and tattoos of Magic Mountain.

It was a new era. The crowd going in wore hickory-stripe bibs, blue work shirts, and environmentally correct T-shirts. They exuded vigor, confidence, Cathedral Hill, *nouveau riche*, law school degrees.

In the corridors touts hawked copies of the movie script. Garrisonophiles bought copies of The Book, biscuit mix tins, and Stoney Lonesome posters. Ratty types circulated through the hordes unloading pirated copies of *Prairie Home Companion* tapes.

I bought cheese curds, turkey legs, praline candy, and herbal tea and settled down in my seat. With less than an hour to go 'til kickoff, a rumor ran amok through the crowd: the vendors had run out of funnel cakes. The mood turned ugly. Then the day was saved. A young man in Amish hat, wire-rimmed glasses, and homespuns stood up and yelled, "Page 134!" The crowd quieted. "Tomato episode! An intellectual curtain descended in the dome. Rustling pages evolved into quiet chuckles, then thunderous approval.

The Amish gentleman raised both arms high above his head and started the Wave. When the cheer subsided, he called out, "Choir, 297." He had the crowd eating Brie out of his hand.

Just then the stadium went dark. You could hear a yuppie drop. On the screen appears a harvest moon, clouds forming three stripes running diagonally toward the center like the left half of sergeant's stripes. A tall grain elevator looms below. Creedence Clearwater Revival sings "Bad Moon Rising."

Quick cut to the exterior of the Sidetrack Tap. The Sons of Knute are leaving after their lodge meeting. Goring each other with the horns of their Hagar-style Viking helmets, they finally get into ranks, link arms, and march down the street singing "Nicolina."

Quick cut to a rising sun. A child looking like Garrison Keillor (played by Garrison Keillor) walks to school kicking a chunk of asphalt. Inside, a Gilbert Stuart portrait of George Washington stares at the schoolroom clock, sees it is 8:30, and nods for the teacher to begin the daily lessons. Closeups show students carving their initials in the desks.

Quick cut to the Chatterbox Café, where the regulars are eating tuna potato chip hot dish and beef commercials. Their wide behinds hang over the stools. Yes, it is a typical day in mythical Lake Wobegon.

Under the subtitle the credits come on the screen: directed by Sydney Pollack; produced by Roman Polansky; book by Garrison Keillor (thundering applause); script by Stephen King; music by Willy and Waylon, the Dale Warland Singers, and Lester Schuft and the Country Dutchmen.

The plot is simple. Fearing extinction of their sect due to television and Donkey Kong, the Sanctified Brethren hire Travis Stotts, a hell fire preacher with television credentials (Geraldo Rivera). Sibling rivalry erupts between the Bunsen brothers at their Ford dealership after Clint (George Carlin), the mechanic half of the team, breaks away from the Lake Wobegon Lutheran Church and joins the Sanctified. He quits putting sawdust in the transmissions of the used cars and starts installing "Jesus Saves" stickers on the insides of all the hoods, trunk lids, and glove boxes.

Manager and car dealer Clarence Bunsen (Tom Cruise) tries to fire Clint. "You can't get rid of me, man," Clint tells him. "I'm a full partner."

Meanwhile Father Emil (Mickey Rooney) down at Our Lady of Perpetual Responsibility Catholic Church brings in new nuns (Molly Ringwald, Cyndi Lauper, and Whoopi Goldberg) to teach at the church school and pep up the flock. Sister Brunnhilde, the head nun (Dolly Parton), fumes.

L. W. Lutheran pastor Dave Ingqvist (Rob Lowe) goes off to play golf while the town burns with indignation. Norwegian bachelor farmers Larry, Darryl, and Darryl (Ed Asner, Bruce Willis, and Richard Dysart) spit and scratch. At the Chatterbox Dorothy (Merle Streep) slams down another order of Surprise Meatloaf. "No imagination. They never ask what the surprise is." Life creeps on at its petty pace.

With conversions every minute, Stotts organizes the Brethren for a rally against the insidious threat of the media. Backsliders sheepishly pitch their record albums into the bonfire: Slim Whitman, Slim Jim, Uncle Ozzie, Wayne Newton, and, yes, even Lawrence Welk. A camera closeup shows Myron Floren's grin dissolving. As the fire dies down, Stotts announces his next campaigns – firing the high school English teacher (Bette Midler) for requiring *Huckleberry Finn* and disbanding the Whippets for defiling Sabbath with ball games, and such lousy ones besides.

Though it's off-season, the Whippet board of directors (Calvin Griffith, Lou Nanne, Harmon Killebrew, and Howard Cosell) convenes at the ballpark. Deposits fall at the First Ingqvist State Bank. Coach Magendanz (Andy Rooney) of the Leonards can't field a team. Children newly converted to the Brethren inform on their parents who had all cheated during last summer's tomato judging.

Meanwhile Nora (Joan Collins) chafes at the monotony of her waitress job at the Chatterbox. "I want to live," she moans, as she throws down her menu with a slap heard through the town. She announces that she is leaving her husband Halmer (Tom Selleck), who has joined the Brethren. Norwegian bachelor farmers scratch and spit in front of Ralph's Grocery.

Nora goes to see Stotts during a three-day rain. He goes through a battle of faith with Nora but finally prevails. She gets out of bed converted. Flushed with victory Stotts delivers a peppery speech to the school board (Kirk Douglas, Burt Lancaster, Charlton Heston, Loretta Lynn, and Tom Hanks). They fire Miss Heinemann, the English teacher, for insubordination.

Stotts has one final goal: conversion of the Norwegian bachelor farmers. At the public square he denounces them for their filthy clothes and the wideness of their combine grain heads. Hundreds of angry citizens march with him out to Vidmar Township. A boy (Garrison Keillor) hurries out ahead to warn the farmers.

The Sons of Knute leave their annual lutefisk supper to head off the Brethren. High on coffee the surviving remnants of L. W. Lutheran, minus Father Emil and Sister Brunnhilde, rally the nuns and children (minus Molly Ringwald, who is doing her hair) and head for Vidmar.

The smell of lutefisk steps up the Brethren pace. Arriving at the bachelor farm house, the Sanctified pelt the unpainted siding with cow chips and sing "A Whited Sepulchre We." Stotts shakes his fist at the dimly lighted front window as a bolt of lightning strikes a cottonwood tree. Nora emerges from the house. "Let's not act so holy, *Reverend* Stotts. Remember how you converted me."

Stotts falls down from a stroke. Children cheer. Knutes nod to each other and say, "Ah, sure." Mickey Rooney and Dolly Parton embrace. The Norwegian bachelor farmers scratch and spit.

Chapter 8
Retirement leads to rut

"Now that you're retired, what do you do all day?" people ask me.

I have to admit at first I was like many retired people, hanging around the post office, eating biscuits at Hardee's, aimlessly wandering around shopping centers looking at cheap foreign made hand tools, watching dogs roam around the neighborhood.

The highlight of the day was the delivery of the St. Cloud *Times*. First, I would check the obituary page to see if I was listed, then I'd read Doonesbury, the sports, editorials, etc. For 15 minutes the time just flew by.

Mondays were big days. Besides waiting for the paper, I had to drag the garbage cans out to the curb. Part of the fun was anticipating when the garbage truck would arrive. There was no reason to carry the cans out ahead of time, thus depriving myself of the thrill of the chase. The rest of the week was a snap, except for Wednesdays, when I had the local paper to read too.

I spent much time on the phone talking to people who wanted to sell me maintenance-free windows, Luce publications, or supplemental medical plans. Many callers wanted to sell my house for me. Others offered to move me out of town. As time went on I organized a routine. I listed all the necessary tasks and prioritized them. Things started to happen.

Being a house husband takes more time than I had anticipated. Vacuuming the carpet takes me about five hours – two to get started, an hour to look for a new bag, and two hours for a nap. Fortunately it doesn't need doing every day, with the kids all living away from home and all.

I also understand better the complaints of women about spending hours slaving in the kitchen. There is a real "hot stove league" for house husbands. "Good food takes time to prepare. Please be patient," is my motto. A supper of fish might take all day. They don't just jump out of the lake into the pan. And now that I'm retired, the wife has quit cleaning them.

Cleaning bathrooms takes the longest – up to three weeks. Throw in a few assorted tasks like bagging up the newspapers, squeezing the last blob out of a tube of toothpaste, watching television, and filing the income tax return, the days just fly by.

I showed early promise for this kind of life. As a ninth grader, I spent an entire semester of wood shop sanding the edges of some boards that were intended for a bookshelf. I wasn't a bit embarrassed at the end of the term when the shop teacher, a dour Welshman, said, "You might as well check those boards back into the lumber room. You haven't taken enough off of them for any charges. I'm not responsible, though, for the wear and tear on your tongue." As a senior I was voted by my class as "Most likely to stand out in his field, whatever field he chooses to stand in." My favorite study methods in college were attending movies and taking long naps.

Now I am better organized. I have two job jars, one for inside duties, one for outside work. Every Monday morning after the garbage cans are at the curb I sit down with a cup of coffee by the big window and start making out a new list of things that have to be done (making lists is considered an indicator of high intelligence). I cut apart the lists, putting each item in its appropriate jar, watch marauding dogs tear through neighbors' garbage bags for a while, then go fishing.

I do set goals for myself. For example, I spend lots of time writing letters: letters of complaint to various stores, restaurants, manufacturers, and legislators. I also devote considerable time answering thin-skinned people who complain about my *Advocate* columns. Some of my letter writing campaigns are more constructive, like my latest project: trying to persuade Prince and Michael Jackson to destroy all copies of "We are the World" and save the starving people by buying Ethiopia.

With warm weather there is much more to do: raking the yard, cutting wood, watching the weeds grow in the garden. There's always fishing or a baseball game to go to. Evenings, I renew my acquaintance with Jim Rockford, the gang at WKRP, and the Cramdens. David Letterman offers philosophical relief. Meanwhile the Great American Novel moves along with its usual leisurely pace.

The garage sale season has arrived. Just last week, I stopped in at the first sale of the year in Annandale. Dozens of women grabbed up cracked dishes and outdated clothes like the alcoholic taking the first drink of the morning. Five years ago I would have been impatient, but now after retirement I don't mind standing in the checkout line with bargains for 15 minutes.

During the years when I was caught up in the competitive, fast-paced material world, I wondered how the hippies could spend hours at a time staring at a grape. How they could spend an entire day at Como Park studying the wisdom in the monkey cages. How they could rap for hours about granola. Now I understand.

A few years ago I viewed a film about the Washoe Indians of California. Their lives were organized around the seasons; their highlight was going into the mountains to harvest acorns, which they used as food in a religious ceremony. Most of the film showed their preparations for the trip. "The Washoe have time," the narrator stated, "time to appreciate, time to savor life." I suddenly understood. In my haste to get things done so I could get more things done, I had lost sight of the important things of life. With retirement, I too have time.

To some people, this kind of life might seem boring and purposeless; it is anything but dull to me. I will never run out of jobs to do, especially if I don't do them in the first place.

Chapter 9

Survival tips for college

"How can you survive on your own? Who's gonna cook for you?" the skeptic asked me uptown just before the school year began. He was astonished that I was going back to college. "I'm not totally helpless," I responded. "No… not totally," he said.

Of course, I'm not really a student – just a student of life. I'm working at a university. From the vantage point of my new job, I'm able to observe collegiate life without the pain of doing the homework. Like many of today's students, I'm no dorm rat, overdosing on lavish meals and having the dishes done for me. I'm on my own living in my own house, master of my fate, captain of my cook stove.

Besides learning advanced expletives to describe my cooking, I've already figured out many valuable lessons about college life:

To save on sheets, sleep two weeks on the one side of the bed, then switch to the other side for a couple of weeks or so. Then, rotate the top sheet to the bottom and vice versa.

Use paper plates instead of china. When using them for soup bowls, use the kind with the dividers and add a second plate underneath. Remember, paper plates don't work on the stove top or in the oven.

The plastic knives always run out before the spoons and the forks. Use a spoon to spread peanut butter, not a fork. It's unsettling to find a plastic tine in your sandwich later on.

The money spent on hiring a dishwashing person is well worth it. Washing dirty pots and pans is demeaning to an intellectual and takes too much of your time.

Don't cook. Munch on free tacos in smoke-filled bars while you watch reruns of *Mork and Mindy*. House cleaning is strictly cosmetic. Unless you entertain frequently, no one will see the mess. If you host a lot of parties, the house will get messed up anyway. Nietzche never wielded a toilet bowl brush.

Go home every weekend to have your wife or parents wash your clothes. It's faster to go home than it is to keep going out to the stores to buy additional underwear, socks and wash cloths.

Don't waste all your time watching television. Movies can augment class lectures. *Crocodile Dundee* revives the archetype of the noble savage. Sly Stallone teaches us how to live the good life. Kevin Costner makes you sensitive. *Pretty Woman* teaches what women are supposed to look like.

Libraries are poor places to study. They lack stereo systems, soft chairs, and video games. You will gain greater insights in the MTV lounge.

If you suffer from terminal muscles in the head, go to college regardless. Physical fitness is in. Wear sweats and roll up the legs to show off those calves.

Learn to spell the name of your major. Employers aren't looking for choir directors or psychologists with lots of opinions that are based on very little studying.

Don't confuse similar pairs: Bob Dylan and Dylan Thomas, George Washington and Washington Irving, Henry Wadsworth Longfellow and William Wordsworth, Freud and fried, the law of supply and demand and sex on demand, "Live Aid" and AIDS.

Question what you hear. No generalizations are true, including these.

Chapter 10
The ubiquitous shoe weed

In mid-summer the wild asparagus dies back and pheasants hatch their young along the Minnesota roadways. A new plant species crops up overnight like mushrooms – the roadside shoe weed. University of Minnesota agricultural experts puzzle over the origins of this infestation, but their colleagues in the Department of Cultural Anthropology have suggested some possible answers.

Scenario 1. A deposed dictator seeks asylum in the one nation that will not exile political crooks. As he and his wife head toward Palm Springs in their stretch limousine, she liquidates her outdated shoes.

Scenario 2. Nine-year-old Johnny realizes the tennis shoes his mother bought for him at a garage sale don't have air valves. He unlaces them, hangs his feet out the side window, and lets nature take its course.

Scenario 3. Eighth grade Rhonda doesn't like the sport shoes her mother bought for her at the mall because they cost less than 95 dollars. She unlaces them, hangs her feet out the side window, and lets nature scatter the seeds.

Scenario 4. A group of Grateful Dead Heads touring the country in their psychedelic 1970 Volkswagon van wile away the time playing strip poker. This also explains the large number of tie-dyed t-shirts along the road shoulders.

Scenario 5. Two teenagers are driving toward Minneapolis. He asks her to prove her love for him. She takes off her shoes and lets him tickle her feet.

Scenario 6. Construction workers in a van pool head home after a hard day's work in The Cities. One gentleman's feet are especially offensive. The others wrench off his shoes and socks and throw them out the windows.

The pipeline welder douses the odorous feet with Pepsi. He turns to the others and says, "You know fellas, it just doesn't get any worse than this."

Scenario 7. To settle a costly labor dispute, a trucking company accepts an offer of free land and a ten year tax abatement to move their operations to South Dakota. Before leaving Minnesota they collect a huge tax write-off for giving their decrepit trucks and trailers to various charitable organizations. As one of these trailers rumbles down the highway under new management, it spews forth donated floor lamps, sofas, *Reader's Digest Condensed Books*, and worn shoes.

Scenario 8. Two rug rats argue over which of the tourist attractions they saw during their 3000 mile trip was the "funniest." The 12-year-old tells her little brother to "put a sock in it" because he thinks the Miracle Mile Video Game Palace was more awesome than Lokksemoe's Garden of Snakes. She forcibly takes off his shoe and backs up her words.

Scenario 9. Shoes are not manufactured in Taiwan and Bulgaria. They are mined. Shoe prospectors cruise the highways looking for paydirt.

Scenario 10. Juniors and seniors initiate the marching band freshmembers on the way to Foley Fun Days. The long-suffering director has to make an emergency stop to buy 10 pairs of white bucks.

Scenario 11. A physical fitness buff pumped up on runner's high doesn't notice he has thrown a shoe and finishes his seven mile run like my son John in the nursery rhyme.

Scenario 12. Decorated with crepe paper streamers and ribald slogans sprayed with Barbasol, a late model Trans Am speeds down the highway toward the Shady Rest Motel. "At least wait till I get my shoes off," she says.

Chapter 11

Hamlet on ice

Seeing the sorrowful expressions on the faces of the losing fans at the end of the boys' basketball tournament, I was reminded of an even sadder moment – the day the ice fisherman stands on the shoreline gloomily staring at the watery edge of the lake, knowing that the ice would support him if he could just get out to it.

Ice fishermen are among the most dedicated of souls. They put up with minus 30 degree windchill, deep snow, and DNR regulations in order to pursue their favorite sport from Thanksgiving until the end of March or early April. Their worst handicap is the melting edges that tear away from the shore of the lake.

You have heard the stories about foolhardy fishermen jumping from ice chunk to ice chunk to nail the big crappies at Lake Sylvia. While most anglers won't take this big a risk, most winter jiggers will go to great lengths to get out on that late ice.

A duck boat can come in handy. The fisherman can push out in the boat through the open water at the edge, then pull hard on the oars and slide the boat up on the shelf of ice. In fact, he may even sit and fish from the inside of the boat out on the ice.

A duck boat helped me out in a different way about five years ago. We were catching the big sunfish along the reed bed in Aarseth's Bay on Clearwater Lake. We had pushed our luck one day too long. We got out on the ice by plank, but we couldn't get off anywhere along the shoreline by the end of that beautiful spring day when the temperature had soared to 68. About five of us would still be standing there today on the ice if a Good Samaritan hadn't come along in a pickup truck with a duck boat in the box.

Why the effort to get out there? Why the risk to life and limb? Well, that's when the big sunnies and crappies hit just below the ice. The fisherman doesn't need mittens. Geese are flying. Red-winged blackbirds trill in the cattail beds. Goldeneyes whistle through the air. Mallards fly by looking for romance.

But at some point the end comes. The danger signs are easily recognized. The angler steps off the shore, wades through boot-high water and steps on the ice shelf, which immediately gives way, immersing him in waist-deep water. Meanwhile, back at the split-entry, his wife is checking through the insurance policies.

Yet, the sportsman knows that the ice is still thick enough to support him if only he can get out to it. He doesn't care that he is wet. The temperature is warm enough to allow him to fish while dripping. After all, he says to himself, you get wet when you take a shower.

Some people build plank systems to bridge the gap between the shore and the solid ice farther out. Of course, if they were structural engineers, they wouldn't have time to fish every day; so planks must be approached with caution. If you ever have to walk someone else's plank, remember the old saying, "He who hesitates is lost."

Several years ago I found myself staring at a plank, wondering if it would hold me up. One plank started from the shore, its other end held up by a concrete block and ended on the ice ledge. I decided to try it. I got to the block and hesitated. It looked all right ahead. About half way across the second plank, I started doubting the black ice at its end. Hamlet-like I stood there. "To go, or not to go?" Just as I had reached "a sea of troubles," the ice gave way, dropping me up to the sternum in smelly, muddy water.

I learned two lessons from that experience: either keep going or don't start out at all, and don't keep valuable papers in your wallet when fishing that time of year.

One of the most dedicated fishermen I ever knew was Ed from Minneapolis. Though plagued with a bad heart, he missed very few days. When the shorelines got bad, he used an extension ladder to reach solid ice. The last spot to get on Clearwater one winter was sheltered by a high south bank. After being out of town for a few days, I headed out there with the pail and jig sticks. Things looked hopeless. The temperature was over 70. I had never fished that late on the ice – April 19. I stood on the high bank. The water along the edge resembled a small river. There out on the ice stood Ed. "They're really biting, Don. Forget it if you don't have a ladder though," he called out to me. I went home fishless and despondent.

Some years ago when the shoreline was getting rotten, my friend Al and I finally located the big sunnies on Clearwater. When we finished up Sunday evening with full pails, we made plans to go out early the next morning. If we started fishing at first light around six, we would have our limits by 7:30 or so. I didn't have to be at school until 8 (8:05 if the principal wasn't standing at the back door of the school with his watch in hand.)

However, the night had been warm and windy. I was concerned about how much the ice might have deteriorated over night. I had stepped in over my boots coming off the lake the previous evening. Still, it was worth a chance.

Arriving at the lake, we took our gear out of the car and walked to the edge. "Looks pretty good," Al said.

"Yeah," I replied, waiting for him to step out first. "Just a minute," I said. "I have a hook caught in my jacket. I'll be with you in a minute."

Al waded through the shallow water, then stepped up on the ice ledge. He took two steps before breaking through. The water was up to his hips. "Not too good here, but it should be solid a little farther out. Just wait a minute. See if I can make it."

He didn't have to tell me to wait. He took three or four more steps. "Whoa!" he yelled as he broke through. The water was now chest high.

"Better come back," I said.

"Yep, I guess it's all up."

He plowed back to shore right through the water like a speedboat coming up to the dock. He climbed up on the bank, dripping the smell of primal ooze. We stood there staring out at the ice that we knew was strong enough to support us. If only we could get out to it.

"Well, time to get the boat and motor ready. We'll get out there as soon as the ice goes out. That's the time to slaughter the big ones," Al said.

Chapter 12
Stamping out sexism

To comply with federal anti-discrimination regulations, I spent the past three weeks desexing things around the house. The cat escaped, but little else did. As I always say, "When the going gets tough, the tough get going."

I began with our rather extensive family library. First of all, I went through every book to eliminate sexually biased words like *man, mankind, chairman, spokesman, humanity,* and *huwomanity.* Violent and sadistic characters like James Bond, Mike Hammer, Philip Marlowe, and Norman Mailer were packed away in boxes and relegated to the back of the closet along with the magazines I buy for the articles, not for the pictures.

Searching for scenes degrading to women, I cut paragraphs, pages, even chapters, out of Hemingway, Mark Twain, Shakespeare, and Erle Stanley Gardner. I saved *Fanny Hill* for historical purposes only. I closely scrutinized seed catalogues and eliminated those that showed women only in the flower beds and men only running the garden tiller.

Not even the children's books escaped. *Grimm's Fairy Tales* was a big offender. I changed half the witches to warlocks and admitted a few lady woodcutters into the forests. An old standard, "The Man with the Blue Light," became "The Woman with the Red Light." Reubenpunzel let down his long beard to draw the fair princess up into the lonely tower in which he was imprisoned.

Then I went through Hoyle to change the sexual bias of card games. I found it disturbing that in every game the king ranked higher than the queen, so I set up the rule that in Five Hundred, Whist, and Pinochle the queen would outrank the king in every other hand. The cribbage player turning up a queen on the cut would receive two points, same as when a jack is turned up.

Then I straightened out the various other games around the house. The checker player now reaching the end of the board would get a piece *personed* or *rulered*, not *kinged*. All sexist words were outlawed in our Scrabble games. Unfortunately, the Game of Life was beyond correction, and I had to throw it out.

Chess was the biggest challenge, only one female piece on each side, although the queen packs quite a wallop. I redesigned the pieces so that the white side would be the female side, the black the male side. The game, thus, would represent the battle of the sexes. The first step was to plan out the new pieces for the white side.

The pawns represented the forward movement of the women's liberation army, the rear corners were guarded by vacuum cleaners; instead of knights on horseback, I invented liberationists with Mace cans. For the diagonal players, I ordained the first female bishops in the newly formed Church of Chess. The king became the queen, the former queen became Gloria Steinem, who would act as prime matechecker.

The black side remained intact, except for replacing the queen with a U.S. congressman from the Deep South. Chess was saved – books, cards, games, what could be left? Looking at my closet, I saw the worst symbols of male servitude. Narrow, wide, square-bottomed, knitted, silk, polyester, denim, striped, checked, polka dotted, glow-in-the-dark, decorated with horses, baseballs, and hula dancers – out went all the neckties.

The sound of a lawn mower coming from outside drew my attention. The mowerperson was a female. Eureka! Why shouldn't I divide up the outside chores so the ladies of our house would have equal opportunity? With youngest daughter Kris soon to be home from college for the summer, this was the perfect time.

I drew up a list of such chores that would be done by the female members of the household: mowing, edging, tilling the garden, pulling weeds, planting trees, spraying weeds, resealing the driveway, washing the car, splitting and stacking wood, pruning bushes, rotating the tires, changing oil, cleaning the garage, and flattening the aluminum cans.

My own list included lighting the barbecue grill, going uptown for the mail, paying bills, buying beer, and twisting lids off pickle jars. My conscience was clear. I had done my bit for feminist liberation. Parity had been met. This is what we all must do. As John Donne said, "No person is an island."

Chapter 13
The compleat angler

One of the most despised character types in America is the amateur, or "rookie." Whatever we do, we must do with grace under pressure, as Hemingway best said it. Leisure time fanatics spend thousands of dollars each year to look polished and professional while jogging or hanging from a kite. Yet people who would never think of playing racquetball in anything less than $200 high top shoes will rush into a fishing trip without ever giving a minute's thought about how to please the huge crowd of spectators who gather at public accesses of popular lakes on opening day to watch, often with binoculars, for the humorous blunders of the uninitiated.

It seems fitting to review before the next opener a few tips that will make the most infrequent angler (research points out that 82 percent of people who fish on opening day don't put their butts on a boat seat the rest of the summer) look like Al Linder.

Bait. Fish bite on anything. Buy everything in the bait shop that swims, crawls, wiggles, or smells. Remember the motto of the American Bait Gatherers and Sellers Association: "You can never have too much bait."

Trailering. If your backing leaves a trail like the writhing of a wounded snake, it's too late to practice. Put your boat in the water before dawn and land it after dark. Pro fishermen put in long hours.

Clothing. Proper dress makes or breaks a fisherman. Never wear clean clothes! Fish can smell laundry soap and are spooked by the flash of a clean-shaven face. Women in your boat will be more attracted to you if you smell like a man. Pay attention to your headgear. Pros wear caps that advertise seed corn or asphalt paving contractors, reruns wear roll-up hats with bucktail spinners hooked in them.

Adaption to opportunity. If you see a boat catch a fish, pull up quickly and move over there.

Weather. Fishermen are not people who "don't know enough to come in out of the rain," they just don't care to. Nobody likes to be called a "fair weather fisherman."

Spawning markers. Stay far away. It's illegal to fish inside them. Fishing near them makes you look like a pinochle player who won't bid on the blind.

Boat behavior. Don't crowd to one side to watch a fishing partner reel in a fish or pull in the beer stringer. Don't lie down while trolling, even when bored. Make sure you have a designated boat driver.

Tackle box. Although people in other boats or on shore can't see your tackle box, your partners in the boat can. A tackle box should have that lived-in look. Try to spill the contents at least once during the day.

Casting. In prime resort areas doctors fill their office walls with hooks and lures removed from unlucky fishermen. Casting etiquette dictates that you must not hook a partner or land a spoon in another boat. If you can't cast, drop a line over the side and jig.

Fishing spots. If you don't have an electronic depth finder, chase other boats. Unless there are lake trout where you're fishing, you're wasting your time in 80 feet of water. However, experienced fishermen will occasionally ignore this advice. One summer I noticed a boat anchored in deep water on Pleasant Lake. I quickly headed over to give them the horse laugh. When I got there, I saw two attractive young females who obviously needed lots of privacy for their sun bath. I decided the walleyes might very well be feeding in 60 feet on such a hot day.

Selecting keepers. The experienced fisherman brings everything in. If you have to come in with an empty stringer, tell the shore loafers you caught 23 northerns but none over your conscience-driven minimum, four pounds. Pros never admit to losing a big one. Above all, don't use the old line, "You should have been here yesterday." This is opening day, remember?

Shore etiquette. Try not to tie up the boat ramp for more than 30 minutes. Don't laugh at someone else's stringer of little one. If you see a big fish, turn away and tell the nearest person about all the big ones you caught last summer. Tell everyone that fishing is never any good on this lake opening weekend because the water is still too cold. While watching people land their boats, chuckle when their vehicles get stuck. Don't help your competitors. Tell them to remember that the "tough get going when the going gets tough." Clean off the milfoil even if nobody is watching.

If you follow all these pointers, you'll look good, like an experienced devotee of Izaak Walton. You too will be a *Compleat Angler*. Who cares if you catch any fish?

Chapter 14

What price leezure?

While engaged in one of those cleaning binges I fall victim to every five or ten years, I saw the old leisure suit hanging in the closet next to my high school letter sweater. What memories it brought back!

The suit caught my attention at Kaplan Brothers store on Franklin Avenue. Its Dijon-mustard coloring, its distinctive chocolate brown stitching, subtly whispered to me. "Relax, enjoy. Throw away those ties," it said.

"I'm 100 percent polyester," it gushed erotically.

That appealed to me. No chance of moth damage if I kept the waxworms in the house too long. Its label said, "Dry clean only." It wouldn't get lost in the laundry room with the dozens of pairs of tube socks and old work shirts.

Then I saw the brand name, Leezure City. I knew I had to have it, no matter what it cost. I put on the jacket and looked in the mirror. Staring back at me, a debonair man of the world – surely no gentleman – pulled on the lever of a nickel slot machine in the Snake Eyes Casino at Reno, with a crowd of admiring grass widows awaiting the big payoff.

Hooked, I took off the jacket. I held it in my hands and admired it from all angles. Its quadruple-vented back was designed to give the wearer flexibility for popping off beer bottle tops. The pockets had no flaps or buttons to inhibit spending sprees.

The euphoria lasted all the way home. I would wear it the next Friday night at the graduation exercises. The guest speaker, a retired president of a long defunct small liberal arts college in Kansas, would crack his three or four jokes that were already old in Lincoln's time, then would begin a long oratorical *tour de force*. Relaxed in my leisure suit, I would doze off, saving my strength for the liquid reception I had planned to attend later that evening.

My first misgivings struck me as I prepared to dress for commencement. All my dress shirts had button-down collars with short points. They just didn't look right with the new jacket. Nor did my penguin golf shirts have the right kind of collar to drape nonchalantly over the jacket's collar. Then I saw an orange Hawaiian shirt circa 1955. It was just the thing – a long pointed collar and the perfect color match.

The gym was a sauna. Steam rising from the hundreds of bodies assembled there obscured the ceiling lights. As one man after another took off his suit jacket, the audience began to take on the depressing appearance of a forest that had been denuded by gypsy moths. Proud of my new suit, I suffered stoically.

The clergyman of the evening delivered the invocation, its shortness a double blessing. The class speakers began. One after another told us that it was an important night, that it was the last time the seniors would all see each other, that their parents had put up with a lot of grief from them (thanks, Mom and Dad), and that they had been through so much together. School really must be a strain. Try being the teacher, I thought.

By this time my pants were glued to my legs and seat. The jacket made me feel like I was rolled in a canvas tent. Steam escaped from around my collar. I took off the jacket, fully exposing the orange and purple orchids. Professor Wilberforce had reached point three of his six-point outline about how the graduating seniors could become better people if they went to church, saved their money, and listened to their elders. So far, I hadn't been rewarded with a single minute of leisure.

The passage of time clouds my memories of the post-graduation party. I must have had a good time, judging from the way the suit looked later. Its waffle fabric was heavily stained, a button was missing from one of the jacket cuffs, the lining was torn. One of the three inside pockets contained a tract titled, "REPENT NOW!"

On the back of the jacket, midway between the shoulder blades, a small hole about the size of a cigarette burn marred its appearance. The jacket wouldn't burn, but it would melt.

The leisure suit never made it to Reno, Hennepin Avenue, or a Halloween costume party. After that graduation night it hung in my closet for ten years until it made its final trip in pursuit of pleasure, to Lindala's Landfill. It never delivered its promised leisure, or *leezure* to be exact. Besides, it didn't look good with my Indiana Jones leather hat or my flannel shirts.

Once in a while I see a few of those polyester jobs at a garage sale. I just chuckle. While I haven't found the answer to the question, "What price leezure?" I know it's more than $39.95.

Chapter 15

The sex life of the vegetable patch

This essay won a National Newspaper award for humor, circulation under 5,000.

Next to a motorcycle parts ad titled, "Mona Lisa Would Smile," the local shopper garden column attracted my eye with its intriguing headline: "The Sex Life of the Vegetable Patch." Before I could read about this corruption, however, I had to leave the house to go to a baseball meeting. I left home confident that no X-rated movies could be filmed in my garden.

During the meeting, my smugness turned to doubt. I hadn't been in the garden for several weeks except to grab a few tomatoes for BLT's. You know how that enthusiasm of April planting fades about the end of May when warm weather weeds start to come, and the rabbits begin their harvest.

When I got home, I hurried out to the backyard, preparing myself for the unknown. Amid the quack grass, was a gigantic singles bar. Steel bands thumped out the rhythms of the bossa nova, long-haired folk singers begged for open revolt against the establishment, alcohol flowed liberally. Frankly, I was shocked. I could put up with a little hanky panky, but this was out of control.

While a few vegetables seemed reluctant to participate in the orgy, the general tone of things suggested the last days of Pompeii. Carrots looked like they were coming off a two week bender, cucumbers gave off the telltale yellowish color of liver failure, green peppers had turned a seductive red. While the Swiss chard looked on, seedy radishes drooled over reruns of *Charlie's Angels*. Hedy Lamarr carried Victor Mature's head on a silver platter.

To find out what was happening, I decided to interview that most conservative of vegetables, the parsnip. I picked out a bearded specimen in a tan trench coat.

"Are things as bad as they seem out here?"

"It's terrible. A complete moral breakdown."

"You seem to be keeping yourself out of trouble."

"Yeah, but it's tough. Those remarks yelled at me all the time – by the tomatoes."

"What are they saying?"

"They say I don't fit in. Worse, they've stereotyped me as a Swede turnip. Everybody knows the Swede turnip is a rutabaga. I'm Norwegian."

"Really? I've always wanted to know that. Tell me, are you people as cold as the media says?"

"No, but we're slow starters. Remember how long it took for those seeds to come up? We finally got going, though, didn't we?"

"That's right, but you don't seem to have much root under you yet."

"No, but our season is a long one. And when we put on the long johns, we can stay in the ground all winter."

"Why is that? You're about the only vegetable that doesn't have to be harvested in the fall."

"Clean living. Look at those green beans over there. Hanging around the bar all the time, living for happy hour and the free tacos. They'll go home with anybody, too."

"They do look a little mottled, but I thought it was bean mosaic."

"Dissipation, plain and simple."

"You don't need much fertilizer. The tomatoes and cucumbers just beg for it."

"No, all I need is some more fish cleanings, and then leave me alone."

Just then I heard some offensive noises – heartburn among the burpless cucumbers.

"Listen to that. Pigs, all of them," snorted the parsnip, whose name I had found out by now was Lars.

"Things are much quieter here in the parsnip row. I admire you for sticking to your principles."

"Yes, I am poor but proud. No backsliding here."

"How are your relatives, the turnips doing?" I asked.

"Not so well. Look at those root maggots at work. And there, that fat one."

"The one with the spaghetti squash hanging all over it?"

"The very one. What does she see in him, you ask."

"I didn't ask."

"She's just after his money. When he turns woody, she'll be right off to look for a new one, a young slim one."

"Lars, what can I do about all this corruption?"

"Pull everything out. Burn all the plants. Plow it up. Just leave my row. You don't have to worry about us parsnips."

"I'll do it. Anything to get rid of this disease. I'll start right away. Well, not right away. I have to cut some wood, go fishing, write the Great American Novel. I'll get around to it as soon as possible."

Hearing no response, I looked over at Lars. His friendly, innocuous smile had turned to a leer. He was ogling a sleek blonde parsnip at the far end of the row. He unbuttoned his trench coat.

Bitterly disappointed, I turned away and started out of the garden, refusing to be turned into a pillar of salt by the promiscuous zucchini. Mona Lisa wouldn't smile if she knew.

I knew then no one was safe from the destructive forces permeating our society. Not even gardening was a harmless pursuit anymore. It would be only a matter of time before the Moral Majority came by with their tractor and plow to obliterate this Frankenstein's monster.

Was my garden even worse than the one written up in the shopper's gardening column? I went into the house to read the article. To my surprise, it was all about pollination, blossom-enhancing hormones, and the value of bees in the pollinating process. Nothing sexy here at all.

Then I knew. My garden *was* immoral, maybe the worst one around. In a fever, I wrote out checks to every television evangelist I could think of. As I was sealing the last envelope, it came to me. My garden isn't any worse than my neighbor's. He just doesn't know. Sure, he talks to his plants, like I do. He just doesn't listen.

Chapter 16

The benefits of beards

During Annandale's 1988 Centennial celebration, I experienced the Walter Mondale syndrome, losing – despite the Las Vegas odds – the Beard Growing Contest, despite three months of careful feeding, watering, and fertilizing.

While congratulations were due Ed Kaz, who grew a two-inch whopper in the allotted time period, I wasn't gracious. The loss was especially bitter considering how the community made a liar out of the Centennial committee's publicity ("You will be greeted by bearded men"). Instead of entering into the spirit of the celebration, most males offered lame excuses for not growing facial hair:

"I grew one in 1971 and my face broke out."

"Beards are too hot in the summer."

"I look terrible in a beard."

"It makes me look old."

"I have the mange."

"My kids won't know me."

"My wife won't like it."

"I'm only six years old."

"I have a bare spot on my chin where Phil stabbed me with the fish spear when we were kids."

"I took some bad drugs in 1968."

"People working the commodities exchange pit do not despoil their faces with facial hair."

"I haven't had any hair on my face since my wife bought that stuff in Mexico to pep me up."

"People won't recognize me in the street."

"These are my husband's bib overalls."

People willing to take a risk would have found out, as I did, that growing a beard has many benefits and few disadvantages, benefits that are financial as well as social.

People asked me, "Isn't it hot with that beard?" Yes, the beard was hot, but it saved me from sunburn. It also helped me in another way. Every time I thought about doing something productive outside, I decided against it because my beard would make my face sweat.

Growing the beard was a time as well as a labor saver. Not shaving for Three months gave me an extra five minutes a day, a total of eight hours that I could have spent reading one tenth of *War and Peace*.

Then there were the financial benefits: shaving cream $.88, razor blades $1.65, hot water $2.32, wash cloths $1.99. Total $6.84.

The greatest benefits were social. The beard gave me anonymity, a plus on days after City Council meetings. But the greatest advantage was with the ladies.

It started at the university where I work. The Dean's secretary eyed my facial hair lustfully, saying, "I'd like to feel it, but I'm afraid someone would see it and I'd be in trouble for sexual harassment."

As the beard got longer, more and more women asked to touch it. Once the weakling on the beach, where women kicked sand in my face, I became the life of the party. Swelled with pride, and a few cold pops, I asked an attractive blonde at the park on July 4th, just before the beard winners were announced, why women like beards so much. "I can't speak for others," she said, "but I like your beard because it reminds me of Grandpa."

It took a week after the holiday before I could bring myself to shave. When I looked at that bare face in the mirror, I asked myself, "How could you ever cover up those attractive features with whiskers?" Still, I plan to grow a beard for Annandale's bicentennial – unless I get a job trading pork bellies.

Chapter 17
Gramma Hammersheit's birthday

Minnesota radio stations have dropped polka music almost entirely from their programming now that old time is trendy. An Associated Press article reports that a band called Polkacide, begun as a joke, has taken California by storm with its amalgam of Polish and Czech-style music that doesn't resemble either type of traditional music.

The beautiful people of San Francisco, dancing to the 15-member Polkacide, whose musicians wear Naugahosen, mismatched plaid suits, and hospital gowns, will never know the atmosphere and ritual of an authentic polka dance like Gramma Hammersheit's 90th birthday dance, June of 1953.

Parking was scarce in the immediate vicinity of the Blossom Ballroom in Springfield, Minnesota. Drivers who could accurately predict the quantity of their drinking backed their cars in for accident-free exit. Those who valued their shiny Oldsmobiles, Packards, and DeSotos parked along the side streets to save the side panels from nicks.

Admission was $1, the average hourly wage for a carpenter's helper or gas station mechanic. A festive crowd flowed through the entrance clutching their *groceries*, paper sacks twisted around bottles of Old Crow or Seagram's Seven. Church clothes were the style: brightly colored dresses for the ladies, suits and ties for the men, though the occasional old timer wore his cleanest hickory-striped bibs.

In those innocent days when drinking was tolerated more as a symptom than a problem, alcohol primed conversation. Booths filled up with relatives and friends who treated each other to setups and lies about how much milk their cows were giving these days just before they would be "dried up" for the summer. Loud and typically German nasal laughs grated on the ears like fingernails scratched across a blackboard.

Just before nine the Babe Wagner band, an eight-piece group, natty in blue jackets, dark trousers, and black ties, took their places on stage. To the strains of the band's trademark, the "Midnight Waltz," Gramma was escorted onto the dance floor by her eldest living son, Florian. Gramma's lightness of foot, surprising because of her 185-pound frame, contrasted to the desperate shuffling of Florian, who was well over 60 and stiff from arthritis and tractor back.

The crowd applauded the pair. As the concertina solo began, the band's announcer called for all the sons and daughters to honor Gramma by getting on the floor. Soon 20 people were dancing. As the band started the "New Ulm Waltz," the call went out for all the grandchildren and great-grandchildren to show their stuff. The floor filled with people who owed their existence to the enjoyment Gramma and her late husband Roman had found in the Biblical admonition "multiply and be fruitful."

After a brief intermission that allowed the band to take a break and the crowd to return to their booths to wet their whistles, the musicians began a polka set of New Ulm-style numbers, "Guido," "Dog House," and "Upside Down." The floor thumped with pounding feet. From the front room bar the dancers shimmered in a haze of cigarette smoke and corn starch dust.

By the next waltz set the band members had taken off their jackets, the seven men that is. The only female in the band, the piano player, looked cool in a stylish white gown. As the concertina played the solo of "I'm Coming Waltz," a slow, nostalgic number, the saxophone section accompanied it with an almost imperceptible harmony. The shuffling feet of the dancers sounded like a procession of grasshoppers through an oats field.

At 10:30 the first fight broke out, right on schedule. All Gramma's children had been given 160-acre farms when they married. Ray thought he had got cheated. The land was swampy, too expensive to tile. Bernie got all prairie flat land. Bernie said, "You'd do better if you quit trying to farm from a barstool." Ray took a swing, missed, slipped, almost fell down. Bernie stood aside. Ray's wife got a hold on Ray and led him to their booth. The relatives didn't show much interest in this battle that had been going on for 40 years since Bernie beaned Ray during a baseball game at Seaforth. One thing you could say in Ray's favor, he sure knew how to hold a grudge.

The singles now looked over each other more closely with intermission an hour away. Gramma's only unmarried son, Cletus, like Marty in the famous Ernest Borgnine role, had long ago quit trying to get girls to dance with him. He perceived himself as fat, sweaty, and dull. Little did he know a dark-haired widow had been eyeing him and his farm, which he had built into a showplace of bright paint and fat cattle through the psychological mechanism of sublimation.

Cletus stood at the bar pouring himself a Schell's beer, ignorant of the conspiracy against his bachelorhood that would break into armed attack next month at the St. Mary's Church bazaar. Almost twenty years from that night he would be celebrating the marriage of his oldest daughter.

After intermission starry-eyed couples returned to the dance hall from their cars. Confessions would run heavy next Saturday, penances stiff. The few Protestants in the gathering, whose consciences would be unrelieved by this sacrament, were doomed to listen to yet another hell fire message from the preacher with the sauerkraut accent. A few marriages had been precipitated, large family farms would be joined, promises of love were spoken, a few young men would join the navy. A mob of sheriff's deputies patrolled the environs. The many fights mostly between young men who hadn't picked up dates to take home, were quickly broken up.

Gramma had quit dancing much earlier in the evening, her soul and temperament in better shape than her legs. She sat out intermission drinking sloe gin with her two daughters and her favorite daughter-in-law Rita. A continual procession of well-wishers brought cards and homage to this matriarch. All agreed they wished they would look as well when and if they lived that long. Most wouldn't though. The next generation's main characteristic was worry. What would happen to their kids who were leaving the farm and small town for work at Honeywell or John Deere in the big city? Was this Korean War a prelude to another worldwide one? Why couldn't people be content with what they had?

At one the dance was over. A large crowd lingered to bid farewell to Gramma. As she got up to go home, she sagged back down in the booth, prey to old age and too many drinks. With Rita on one side and Flavia on the other, Gramma again raised herself up, a worldly grin on her face. "I sure know how to have a good time, not?"

"Stay between the ditches," Bernie said to Ray, arm around him. Ray said, "Your flax field looks good. Not as good as my barley though." "With all the beer you drink, you should raise good barley," Bernie replied. They both laughed.

Next Saturday most of the same crowd would return here for the wedding dance of Rosemarie Kubes and Jerome Pelzl, with music by the Blue Gordon band. Rosemary is Gramma's grandniece. Jerome is Ray's wife's sister's boy.

Chapter 18
Surviving mate's hospitalization

While it's no picnic to recuperate in the hospital after open heart surgery, things aren't easy for the significant other who has to take care of the detail work while making daily trips back and forth to visit the patient.

Trying to find something interesting on the car radio was a daily struggle. Worse were the drivers on Highway 55, who turned the road into a combat zone. One day a gentleman driving in a green van decorated with Himalayan scenes, gurus and all, rode my tail between Buffalo and Loretto. Unable to pass because of slow moving traffic and frequent no passing zones, he would drop back slightly, then gun it and zoom right up against my rear-view mirror.

Who was this person? I wondered. A high-powered business executive, stockbroker, realtor with the IDS Building listing, a candidate for governor? There couldn't be anything so important to get that worked up about.

I wrote down his license number, intending to send him a copy of *Walden*. At the Loretto stop light, his tires squealed as he pulled his car off the highway and into the gas station. Yes, there is something that important, I realized.

My own driving required some reorganization. The first trip to Minneapolis and back took a tank of gas. When I got home, I sat down and assessed the situation. My philosophy of driving had always been to drive like heck and then slam on the brakes. After a few trips I learned to pace myself, watch the lights more closely, and avoid quick stops and starts.

The strategy worked. Gas consumption went down considerably. Yet there was an uncomfortable feeling that I wasn't fully taking advantage of the 50-cent-a-gallon saving over last year's gas price. In one way I was beating the system, in another, I was losing.

Pumping gas one day, I shoved the nozzle too far into the neck of the gas tank. The nozzle jammed, the coil of wire catching somewhere inside. As I worked on the problem with a screwdriver, it hit me. Did I really want the price of gas to go down? I owned 500 shares of an Oklahoma wildcat drilling company. Every time the price of gas goes down, they cap another well. Too busy to worry about J.R., I knew that if the price of crude didn't go up soon, I could make a rec room decoupage out of that stock certificate.

Things weren't going well at home either. Dirty laundry piled up in spite of my efforts to conserve by wearing a shirt three days at a time. Clean underwear and socks joined the endangered species list. Towels ran short. I had never stolen towels from motels, but I started to regret my strict moral principles. I took the last towel out of the linen closet. Staring me in the face was its inscription, "Grandpa."

I knew it was time to wash a load of clothes. Well, it's not hard to operate a washer and dryer, even for a macho type guy. The hitch came later when it was time to fold things and put them away. For some reason, I ended up with 16 unmatched socks. It was time to improvise. I folded socks together in unmatched pairs. Who looks at both feet of another person at the same time?

Dishes were another problem. While I wasn't home to prepare many meals, dishes still piled up in the sink. I switched to paper plates and plastic forks after I had spent a whole day with my hands in dish water. Forget about Greenpeace. I didn't want dishpan hands. To make matters worse, the microwave was on the blink. I couldn't use those quick convenience foods that taste like the cardboard they come in. As I heated a can of soup, I wondered why someone doesn't invent a line of stew pans and frying pans that set right on top of a burner, then can be thrown away after the food is cooked and eaten out of them.

One day before I could get out of the house a group of itinerant vacuum cleaner salesmen arrived at my door, intent on shampooing my carpet and selling me a new vacuum. I hesitated. "Well, things are in a little mess right now with my wife in the hospital and all. There's quite a bit of stuff piled around on the floor. All these important projects I'm working on. You understand."

"That's all right," one drummer said. "We can move stuff aside and then put it right back. We always clean a floor in sections anyway. It's easier than moving all the furniture."

I tried not to show my excitement. I hadn't vacuumed for several weeks. They worked for a while. One guy moved assorted piles of city council material, story outlines, and newspapers that I intended to read some day when I got around to it. The other pushed the vacuum. Then he shut off the machine to change bags and asked. "How often do you vacuum?" I answered, "Well, not every day but quite a bit." They finally left with no sale. The living room was still one step ahead of what the Vandals had done to Rome.

I learned a few things during those weeks when I was on my own: how to change light bulbs, install toilet paper on the spindle, dye white T-shirts, and bake frozen pizzas. It was nice to have Marlys home again, but our nine-year-old cat was just as happy. He was tired of bagged food, and I won't dish out the canned stuff. The last time I handled such foul-smelling material I had a pitch fork in my hand instead of a spoon. Now I have to hustle to get the yard cleaned up before the annual city inspection. Thank goodness they can't come in my house to check out my housekeeping.

Chapter 19

Garge Sales – there oughta be a law

"They sure aren't what they used to be," a guy said, as we stood at 7:30 in front of a garage shut up as tight as an old German's wallet.

"They sure aren't," I replied. "We run around from one sale to another, and we're lucky to find one good bargain the whole day."

We waited five longer. A crowd formed, and the mood was ugly. "Why can't they get up in the morning?" I asked. "The ad said 8 o'clock. They oughta know people are gonna be here by 7:15. There oughta be a law." The minute hand of my watch moved as slowly as a teenager grows up. I kept reminding myself of the biggest lesson I had learned from the years of garage saleing: don't buy another corn popper.

The garage sale is the last human activity unregulated by state or federal law, and it's about time that changes. While we might give lip service to rugged individualism, deep down those of us who have devoted a lifetime to chasing bargains are sick and tired of unscrupulous garage sale robber barons. We expect to get ripped off at the mall, but not at the neighbor's.

In the garage sale industry, truth in advertising is a joke. It's *caveat emptor* for the unwary who can't decode the classifieds:

"Gigantic garage sale" – it's 30 x 40.

"It all must go" – to the dump.

"Free coffee" – and inflated prices; there's no free lunch in America.

"We sold the cabin and are moving to Arizona by car" – the kids and grandkids have taken everything but the pocket fisherman, a card table full of tools made in Sri Lanka, a nine-foot rack of leisure suits and polyester stretch pants, and the dog's rocking recliner chair.

"Nine family sale" – these nine neighbors haul the stuff around from place to place all summer.

"First time ever" – this virgin used to haul her junk over to her sister-in-law's.

"Garge Sale" – don't even consider this one. There oughta be a law.

It's hard to find a bargain anymore. When a family has a sale every year, sometimes twice a summer if they don't unload their junk the first time, even a bag lady would have trouble finding a good deal at the next one. When the sale is legitimate – lots of goods, good prices, a seller too weak to refuse any offer – things get vicious. People crowd each other, take things out of each other's hands, and try to cut deals on fifty cent items, while the seller is selling something twice.

Still the hope is there, and the legends linger. The free box. The ten-dollar Strad. The 1931 Johnson Flipper Frog, in its original box, for a quarter. The five-hundred-dollar antique camera for three dollars – "Would you take a buck and a half?" the good garage saler asks. And gets it.

The buyers have changed too. It used to be a bunch of people going around looking for things they didn't need, couldn't afford, couldn't identify, and wouldn't have room to store. That way they'd have to put on their own sale the next summer. Now, half the buyers are professionals who sell at polkafest flea markets, and the principle of too many buyers chasing too few goods reads like a bad Econ 101 textbook. The days of the two-bit pliers are gone forever. There oughta be a law.

It's a jungle out on the highways too. You can easily spot the people on the road when they're headed for a garage sale. The car wears an anxious look and a bumper sticker that says, "This car brakes for all garage sales." The Department of Motor Vehicles doesn't keep statistics on the number of accidents caused by garage saleing, but everyone knows it's the third largest cause of traffic accidents, only trailing drinking drivers and stupidity. Defensive driving won't keep you out of trouble. You have to be lucky.

The wary shopper learns to stay away from certain items: transistor radios, Lawrence Welk albums, closed face reels, home-canned sauerkraut, and men's clothing (women trade in their clothes when they get tired of them, teenagers after they've worn them once, but men get rid of their stuff when they start to rot).

So many times I've been forced to resell bad popcorn poppers, the air kind. One didn't heat up at all, one dimmed the house lights, another had the air pressure of Camel Joe's lungs. Yet I was assured every time that "they work great." There's always a good excuse for unloading them. "My husband likes his popcorn with lots of grease," or "Clyde's got pouches." Face it, at garage sales it's consumer fraud. There oughta be a law.

Last summer I asked a few women why garage sales are so popular. The answers were predictable. It's a good chance to clean out the closets, Jerry won't give me any spending money, the kids can trade their school clothes with their friends, my husband is a pack rat, this is a good way to get the best of a bunch of dumb men, it's a good time – we can get together and smoke with our girlfriends.

She and her three friends were smoking up a storm. "How come so many women are smoking these days, when at the same time their husbands are quitting?" I asked. The answer came in a hurry. "They're quitting, and they're driving us nuts. That's why we're smoking."

About four o'clock on a hot Friday afternoon I arrived at a garage sale in a nearby town. It was the worst time to show up. The sale had been going on since eight Thursday morning, and it looked like Mother Hubbard's cupboard. The seller was alone and talkative. We discussed pleasantries for a few minutes. Jack works third shift, the kids were at grammas. Then she pulled the bottom of her shirt out of her Wranglers and fanned her face with it. The time was ripe to ask her why she likes garage sales. She smiled voluptuously, "For some women they're like chocolate. And not fattening," she added, scattering morals with every wriggle. "Well, I don't see anything I want," I said. "I mostly look for fishing stuff."

In her case, there already is a law.

Chapter 20

Our humane treatment of cats

Our trouble with cats started again one day when a neighbor boy remarked, "Your cat had kittens, huh?" Superciliously I chuckled, then dropped the big one. "That would be quite an achievement. He's a tom." With the patience that kids have to use when explaining the facts of life to adults, he replied, "No, your other cat. Look in your old truck."

We didn't have another cat, but I knew what he meant. A stray black cat had inhabited our garage since the fall, surviving cold, insufficient food and water, and my efforts to capture it. A few weeks later I had seen it in an imminently expectant mood. Then it disappeared. Refusing to allow my garage to be used as a laying-in hospital, I shut the doors. I put the cat out of my mind, only occasionally wondering what neighbor would soon be inflicted with a litter of kittens.

As I opened the door of the 1961 International Scout, the vehicle with the sliding window that I suddenly realized was so convenient for cats, I was plunged into the Oligocene epoch. Kittens scattered in every direction, hiding under the seat and beneath the dash. The mother cat greeted me with an unfriendly hiss. Once more I was faced with the problem of getting rid of a bunch of cats.

Although we have turned away many free-lance cats, we invited the first one in to be a companion to our kids, who were then quite small. A flower child who refused to obey the conventions of traditional morality, such as using the litter box, Christmas soon made the trip to the Humane Society in St. Cloud.

The next cat was more to my liking. A big, black stray, he loitered around the porch all summer. When the weather got cold, he moved into the house, where he discovered my favorite chair. He developed a preference for taco chips and beer. He also loved to eat fish. When I brought home a pailful, he would devour two or three sunfish, heads, tails, bones, and all. He stayed almost a year, disappearing during that early November lull between boat fishing and tiptoeing out on thin ice. We figured he must have found a better fisherman or moved into a saloon.

In the meantime, a friend had become overrun with cats. He stopped over one day and picked me up on the way to St. Cloud. He had two grocery boxes filled with cats and kittens. A gray tiger cat rested on the back seat. "Don't worry about that one. She's tame. She'll ride just fine that way."

Arriving at the Humane Society, he stopped the car and carelessly opened the door. "Wait!" I yelled, but it was too late. The cat streaked out the door and headed for the adjoining scrap metal yard. All we could hope for was that it wouldn't run into Jim Croce's "junkyard dawg." We each picked up a box of cats and walked to the door, where we were greeted by a stern admonition: "$500 fine for abandoning animals."

A few years ago, our family acquired another cat by the walk-on method. By this time, I started wondering why so many cats came to our doorstep. Water torture brought out that Maija and Kris had been putting out cat food on the back porch. I was adamant and refused to allow the new cat in the house. Still, it hung around.

One blustery winter day the cat was watching me load wood when it somehow got under the pickup's back wheel and broke a leg. I couldn't afford to take it to a vet. Besides, this didn't drink beer or do much of anything else. Soon I was on the road again.

As I was slipping and sliding along icy Highway 24, I worried about whether the Humane Society would like this cat. After all, it was injured. I also worried about running off the road and dying in a snow drift, knowing that while I was toes up the cat still had eight lives left.

After a two-hour 25-mile trip, I arrived at the animal shelter, where the attendant felt sorry for me and agreed to take the cat off my hands for a small donation.

Our present cat, a black tom, is another unsolicited member of the family. He does what cats do best – eat a lot, sleep, stretch, and yawn frequently, make many in and out trips day and night, and demand attention. Accidentally misnamed Katie, he likes to hunt and bring home carcasses of disgusting tiny swamp animals. Unlike our previous black cat, Spades, he will not eat fish cleanings, preferring northern livers and crappie fillets.

Like most cats, Katie always moves slowly through doors, especially during twenty-below weather or in the mosquito season. Cats are the royalty of the animal kingdom and must be processed with all due pomp and circumstance. Still, he's our cat, and we are stuck with him.

Now we have a whole family of cats. As I look out the windows this morning toward the garage, they are all out. The mother cat lies in the grass switching her tail back and forth as the kittens run at it and grab it. Kittens tumble over, wrestle with each other, chase dragon flies. I count them – two gray ones, a black one, another gray one, two more black ones, another gray one, more black ones, no, I counted them before. I don't know how many there are. I empathize with the problems of the Census Bureau in these days of the transient family.

Instead of chasing them away, Katie dozes indulgently on a nearby woodpile. We must solve our own problem. To keep the bird population from extinction, we are now feeding the cats all they can stand. Eventually they may become tame enough for capture, but at present they instinctively sense the pens of the Humane Society.

Chapter 21

The hot weather types

A long hot summer leads, unfortunately, to many divorces and/or murders, but it also gives us the opportunity to reexamine human character types and their reactions to Minnesota's version of the 20-mile forced march with full pack.

The Philosophers. "It's not the heat but the stupidity. Take it easy, work slow. Take long lunch breaks. Rome wasn't built in a day. In four months, we'll be pushing out the ice fishing shacks."

The Loungers. Outside the local bars at 8 a.m., awaiting the opening call, they recite Omar the Tentmaker's immortal lines from the Rubaiyat:

And as the cock crew, those who stood before the tavern shouted –

'Open then the door! You know how little while we have to stay,

And once departed, may return no more.'

Omar's boys left the oasis on camelback at closing time. Let's hope these modern hedonists lose their car keys.

The Old Swede Farmers. "Eat lots of salty sausage, drink lots of hot coffee, chew snoose, and work like heck."

The Teenage Style-Mongers. Garbed in flowered Hawaiian shirts and blue and white jams, heads topped with spiked hair, they spend so much time avoiding motorcycle gangs they don't even realize how hot it could be.

The Air-Conditioned. They escape the cool house to get into the cool car to go to the air-conditioned mall and comfortable movie house. They idle the car for up to an hour while waiting for family members to run errands.

They rub it in to the unfortunate. "No air conditioning? Man, you must be suffering!"

The Sweaters. Perspiration pours down their faces, their glasses are steamed, their shirts soaked, their shoes go "squish, squish." Bravely, they tell us, "No, I'm not so hot. As long as I can sweat, I'm okay. Let's have another cup of coffee."

The Elderly Neighbors. "Gee this warm weather feels good."

The Vacationers. Attired in almost decent beach clothing, they foray into the supermarket, turning every red-blooded young man's career goals toward stocking grocery shelves and sweeping floors. And a few disreputable old guys too.

The Sloshers. The noisiest of the hot weather types, on a typical day they suck down eight or ten diet pops, six glasses of water, two root beer floats, and a 12-pack of beer. Their stomachs sway from side-side as they walk. Their every word is accompanied by the gurgling of gentle rapids moving over flat rocks.

The 60's Remnants. "Is it hot, man? Don't ask me."

The Rest of Us. We hide like rats, departing home sweet home only long enough to buy bread and milk. We ride it out watching soap operas and government scandals. We close the drapes all day long to keep the sun out. We try to read newspapers in the teeth of the gale created by numerous big fans scattered throughout every room. We drink gallons of ice water. We eat canned sardines and cottage cheese lest we heat up the house by cooking a real meal. We complain constantly. We know this is the hottest summer ever. We know no one else is as hot and miserable. We live and die with the Twins. We watch Arctic films on educational television. We read Jack London tales of the Klondike. We develop cabin fever. We complain.

We resolve to start out the next day doing things. We write out lists:

1. Mow lawn

2. Weed garden

3. Paint house

4. Clean house

5. Wash car

6. Transplant irises

7. Water lawn

8. Lose weight

9. Walk

10. Jog

11. Sit in the shade

The next morning we start on the list. With number 11.

Chapter 22
The law of the corn

They sprawl in front of the high school, their clothes ragged and filthy. Not the cast the *Night of the Living Dead*, these unwalking wounded have survived one more day of the worst job in America except the Presidency. These corn detasselers are waiting for a ride home, their feet sore, legs tired, lips sunburned, and minds numb from a day spent trying to dredge up an excuse so good they never have to come back to the fields again. They've outlasted soaking dew in the morning, 90-degree heat and corn rash in the afternoon, and overheated bologna sandwiches. They've lived through another day of the greatest teenage horrors: taking orders from an older person and no TV.

In farm country of the Upper Midwest this is the first job for many kids. I was thrilled when an older guy, a college student no less, asked me to be on his crew. I was 13, I'd never had a job, and the pay was good – 60 cents an hour.

What a snap! Six of us stood on a machine high above the corn, each responsible for our own row. We leaned down from our little platforms and pulled out the tassels as they greeted us. Occasionally we missed one, and the eagle-eyed driver ordered us to jump down and run back to get it. Then we had to catch up on foot as the machine crept onward. Back on our perches, we daydreamed about the Brooklyn Dodgers and an ice-cold Dad's root beer in its thick brown frosty bottle.

I learned valuable lessons at the fields. Corn rows are long, lunches should have lots of sweet stuff, you need a three-bladed knife for mumblety-peg, and older kids like to pick on the greenhorns.

Then torrential rains descended, grounding our machine. We joined up with a gigantic crew of girls – the horrid *walking crew*. They had been only a rumor, but now we found out why our job on the machine was so easy. We were just picking the leftovers. These girls were responsible for really cleaning out the fields.

The rows were endless, the corn towered high above. Sensitive male skin itched from pollen and leaf cuts. As my 12-inch work boots sank to the tops in mud, I remembered the *Suspense* radio drama about the man who drowned in quicksand. The "squish," "squish" from the suction as we lifted each foot sounded like the call of the slough pumper. We finished the day, but not without griping that would put a seasoned army company to shame. I had learned the misery of women's work.

Just out of high school I got the opportunity to head up a girls' walking crew. The pay was great – a dollar an hour – so what if I hated to walk? I was the boss! Not that I had to be. The girls were tough. I just had to stay out of their way and mark down their time in a DeKalb notebook. I learned valuable lessons in the fields: girls can swear with the best of muleskinners, they eat bigger lunches than guys, and the female anatomy looks good close up. When it got hot, it was suntan time, and the shirts came off. "Life's a beach," I thought. I also learned not to walk back to check up on someone who was lagging far behind.

Fifteen years later I had accumulated a wife, four kids, and two college degrees. Not a very original thinker, I was back in the corn fields, this time working for Norm Planer's operation near Annandale. I had traveled a long way in my lifetime, over 100 miles.

This was a traditional operation in that the rows were endless, the corn was tall, they didn't use machines, and the tassels had to be pulled with no leaves, or at least no more than one. After all, twenty percent of the moisture and nutrients came through the top leaves, we were told by the supervisors of the Wadena-based contracting company that supplied seed corn to Funk's. This argument didn't impress the detasselers at all because it slowed them up and diverted their attention from what they did best, throwing tassels and laying down at the ends of rows.

Eventually I accumulated six or seven seasons of experience in those fields. It was a good job. I started at five dollars an hour, and all I had to do was keep twelve or fifteen boys from demoralizing each other. I had plenty of time. Everybody knows teachers don't have anything to do in the summer. And by the end of June I was already starting to miss being around students.

It wasn't always fun. The first time or two through the fields, tassels were thick, and we crept on our petty pace. Some of the nicest kids around school were the most pathetic workers. I cried "Excelsior!" but many young boys succumbed to the law of the corn.

To kill time, I watched the ground for the telltale leaves, evidence of a careless job. I studied lady bugs, corn smut, and hermaphrodites. I enjoyed watching the older kids pick unmercifully on the younger ones because I was the biggest kid.

Starting off a new crew was like trying to break mules. Why did they throw tassels? Why did they pull the tops off plants? Why did they move so slowly? How could they miss so many? How could they walk right by them? Why didn't those who got to the end of the row go back and help somebody else finish? How did they learn to swear like that? How could I learn to swear like that?

They asked their own questions. Why couldn't they smoke? Why couldn't they chew? Why was the pay so low? Why was it wet? Why was it hot and dusty? Why couldn't they walk barefoot? Where was the water? When was it break time? When was it lunch time? Why couldn't they fight? Why couldn't they beat up the crew leader?

Though I hid it well, I was embarrassed. Here I was – thirtysomething. I thought I could gripe like a career foot soldier, but I couldn't carry the shoes of these kids. I studied them and tried to learn.

The greatest incident of my detasseling career came the day Freddy (assumed name) took the big dare. Detasselers love to stone gophers, rabbits, birds, anything that moves, but frogs were the best because they were the most helpless. The boys pulled their legs off, squished them, prodded, poked, and choked them. The frogs took it like Dukakis in the

1988 campaign.

Someone – a future Presidential speech writer, perhaps – was inspired. "Freddy, I dare you to swallow that frog you're skinning." Freddy stared a minute, intrigued by the challenge. "Okay, if everybody gives me a buck." General agreement all around. Of course, nobody carried money in their filthy jeans. They all agreed to bring the money the next day. Except me. I stood there like Jack Benny. I was the boss. I deserved my entertainment for free.

Freddy pinched the frog in his right hand, tilted his head back, and lowered it into his mouth. Then he jerked the frog back. A false start. Those who didn't want to lose a dollar were relieved. The rest of us were disappointed. Then he lowered the frog again, this time halfway into his mouth. He jerked it back again. We shrugged at each other. We knew he had no intention of swallowing any amphibian that day unless he had jambalaya in his lunch box. I turned away. "Wait!" Freddy cried out. "I was just playing around."

Again, the frog began its tour of Freddy's oral passages, but this time he let go and gulped. With a final kick of its legs, the frog disappeared. Freddy smiled his Cheshire cat grin. Joe and Andy ran in the corn rows and threw up. Freddy went on sick call that afternoon. He was AWOL for two days. When he came back, nobody had money. He never did get paid, but I suspect he was pleased anyway. After all, virtue has its own reward.

Chapter 23

Minnesotans say yes to 55

"I want to live long enough to see my new granddaughter (Savanna Kristine Hanson, 7 pounds, 4 ounce, born Jun 17; our family's first Norwegian)," the wife said, seizing the car keys away from me with all the authority of an old time bartender wrestling away the chance to drive from a habitual bar drunk.

So we set off for Fergus Falls via Minnesota Interstate Speedway I-94. As the big Buick settled in at the new 65 mph speed, I sat back to catch up with a week's news in the St. Cloud *Times*.

The first evidence of the new highway pace was ominous. An orange Corvette with the license plate "I JET" flew past. That's nothing I thought. "I Don," I said to Marlys. "You Jane. If I had a sports car, I'd show off too." I concentrated on the major league box scores.

It was hard to keep my mind on statistics, though, with the continuous stream of cars passing us up. We were lapped by numbers, birds, horses, celebrities, and foreign cars bent on conciliation, accord and reliance. Even a 1979 fish. "Put the pedal down," I said, as an ancient Dodge Charger with battle fatigue rattled past. The Charger smiled and waved. My chauffeur ignored me.

Brooding over a St. Louis Cardinal loss, I looked up from the newspaper. "My God, they're passing us on both sides!" I screamed. Not to worry. It was the St. John's exit with its extra lanes. Vehicles older than my favorite fishing rod and reel were leaving the speedway at 70 and faster.

My last frazzled nerve snapped as a group of modern voyagers swept by, canoeless. The scene was out of an older, more innocent, energy-lush era. The driver, male of course, chewed gum, puffed on a cigarette, and dangled a toothpick out of one corner of his mouth. His female companion in the front seat read *House Beautiful*. Two sub-teens in the cargo hold pummeled each other with water skis. "Make military components, not love," a bumper sticker proclaimed. "If I can see the whites of your eyes, you're too damn close," warned another.

I gave up on the paper and leaned forward, better to appreciate this motorized caravan bent on a weekend of depleting Northern Minnesota of its fish population and beer supply.

When the new speed limit was proposed, opponents warned that motorists would be confused. They would try to drive 65 on all the highways, not realizing that the new law would be a dispensation meant only for rural interstates. They weren't confused on I-94. They understood clearly that 65 was a minimum speed. The slow lane had gone the way of the covered wagon and the Edsel.

It was a relief to get held up in Fergus Falls by the annual Scandinavian Days parade. Bands and floats processed at a pace considerably below 65 mph. These were the first moving objects I had seen all day obeying the speed limit.

The return trip was equally as frazzling as the first lap. Cars, pickup trucks, and vans sped past our car, whose cruise control was regulating our speed at 65. Semis hauling grain, waferboard, and four-wheel drive tractors played moto-cross. The under-manned state highway patrol was nowhere in sight.

The 65-mph speed limit is the most effective piece of law ever enacted in Minnesota. The governor accomplished with one stroke of the pen something all our legislative genius has not been able to do: make a decision that everyone can accept. It certainly was unanimous on I-94 that Saturday. Everyone was driving at least that fast.

Chapter 24

The college blues

In the fall of 1984, we took Carl to Macalester College for freshman orientation week. The welcome ceremony in Weyerhauser Chapel was impressive: the grand march of professors in their colorful robes led by a bagpiper, greetings from college president Robert M. Gavin, Jr. Even more impressive, though, was the sight of the students moving into the dorms.

Grand Avenue was dotted with rental trailers. Family retainers staggered under the weight of trunks and suitcases. Several people helped a girl carry in a queen-sized mattress and bed frame. With visions of *Animal House* and *Revenge of the Nerds* dancing in their heads, parents clung fearfully to their children.

These safari-like efforts were far removed from my matriculation at Mankato State College in 1957, when I arrived on the now abandoned Lower Campus with three shirts on hangers and a small suitcase stuffed with enough underwear and socks to last until Friday afternoon, time of Exodus for the majority of students at Suitcase U.

Laundry was a big problem for most of us, especially when we decided to stay on campus for occasional weekends. Men didn't wash their own clothes. One of my friends solved the dilemma by mailing his dirty clothes home each week in a cardboard suitcase. It wasn't until my junior year that I accidentally stumbled onto a laundromat while walking from my off-campus apartment to class one day. I didn't like the smell and the heat. It was time to find a serious girlfriend.

College was a great place to develop new stereotypes. Korean students were all named Kim. Students from Iran and other Mideastern nations had lots of money, hence great appeal to the co-eds. Students from The Cities were all high class, sophisticated people who drove MG's. Art majors wore berets and funny little beards. "Ignorance is bliss," someone once said.

Later on reality set in. An Iranian was arrested for trying to rob a supermarket. I learned that not all teacher candidates were gifted intellectuals. The college professors who spent the most time in the student union drinking coffee and spouting bull session philosophy with the undergraduates were the ones who did the least in their classes and more often than not were the people who taught Education 301.

However, this spiritual defoliation came long after I was sent from home with a deck of cards and a handshake, encouraged in the true spirit of Lake Wobegon to "make something out of myself." Those were the Horatio Alger days when a year at a state college cost only about a thousand dollars and the streets were filled with millionaires' daughters who needed rescuing from sports car attacks.

First order of business for a freshman was to get acquainted, and there was no better place than the men's dorm. Them were two of the first people my roommate and I met. North Them bid no trump a lot. South Them held the joker more than his fair share of the hands. Admiring Them's style of 500 playing, my friend and I made plans to play cards with Them the next afternoon.

Day after day we played at one o'clock. Without ever asking Them, I assumed that Them had all morning classes, same as we did. Shortly after fall quarter grades came out, Them's chairs were empty for the first time. It was then that we met Them's morning session opponents and realized the truth – North and South had failed to attend any classes and had been dropped from school.

Even though we had played every day for a whole quarter, I had never gotten around to asking Them their names. As an English major, and presumably literate, I marked score every game. My roommate and I were always Us, our opponents always Them. I asked my partner if he knew Them's names. "I dunno," he replied. "Where are Them from?" I asked. "Who cares?" he answered, scanning the lounge for new competition.

College days were filled with decisions – what to major in, what professors to avoid, whether to take college algebra or bonehead math, is *Catcher in the Rye* a more important book than *Peyton Place*, whether to order Italian sausage or pepperoni.

Today's undergraduates, who live in Liberty Hall, probably wouldn't believe the restrictions colleges in the 1950's placed on their students, especially the females. Instead of a choice between smoking or non-smoking dorms, men's or women's or mixed halls, in those days there was the men's dorm and the women's dorm. In their infinite wisdom, college officials allowed male students to roam free, while co-eds had to check in and out at night, had to be in the dorm by 10 p.m. on weekdays, 12:30 on weekends.

With a feverish desire to play parent, colleges required Orientation Class, in which bored students read newspapers or dozed as the Dean of Women lectured on the dangers of going steady. Campus card tables were especially busy at 3 p.m. on Thursdays, when a cut meant both the avoidance of paternalism and the excitement of bidding ten hearts on two tricks, the blind, and a partner.

Today, colleges are more willing to let their students grow up on their own; regulations are few, academics are stressed. Card playing is becoming a lost art. I wonder whatever happened to Them.

Chapter 25

Football in the land of the bard

Editor's note: This essay originally appeared August 13, 1986, shortly after the USFL disbanded. The premise and details have proved to be eerily accurate, and have not been changed from the original.

Tired of reading about coronations and royal weddings? Weary of speculating over whether or not the royal "We" are pregnant? Do you hate the Beatles, the Rolling Stones, punk rock, any rock? Let's purge ourselves of all this anger and pent up hostility by a nefarious act of revenge – let's send the USFL to England.

This ersatz league has announced that it won't be operating this fall, a victim of NFL, anti-trust violations, they say. Here they are, all dressed up and no money to pay the bills. They should take a look at the tremendous success of the recent historic battle in London between William "Refrigerator" Perry's Chicago Bears and America's team, the Dallas Cowboys.

With 82,699 gawkers jammed in Wembley Stadium, munching on fish and chips and tea and crumpets, swilling warm ale, it looks like the land of Churchill has enough fan interest to support a struggling league like the USFL.

Think of the possibilities for team names. The Avon Bards, the Nottingham Sheriffs, the Plymouth Rocks, the Winchester Cathedrals, the Canterbury Pilgrims, the Newcastle upon Tyne Colliers, the Reading Books, the Sherwood Hoods (or Merry Men), the London Queens.

Let's not swell our unemployment lines with ex-football players with two and a half years of credits in Sports Information Writing and Field Team Games Performed with One Hand. While Herschel Walker, Doug Flutie, Jim Kelly, and a few others might move right into NFL lineups, the rank and file are doomed to a life of pick and shovel labor and slow pitch softball. No, send them to Shakespeare country.

More important than balancing our Common Market trade deficit is the Howard Cosell problem. Actually it's two problems. His problem since getting squeezed out of Monday Night Football is finding something to do. He has even sunk to covering baseball, a sport he once considered as interesting as watching paint dry.

The other Cosell problem is ours. Now we have to read his columns, gigantic purple passages that wreck revenge on Pete Rozelle and all television executives who are too stupid to hire him.

Moving the USFL to Merry Old would be the flip side of the Lend Lease program. During World War II we sent them bombers and ships. They returned the favor with Boy George and David Frost.

Let's carry revenge one step farther. Viking General Manager Mike Lynn gets my vote for USFL commissioner in England because of his years of expertise at holding down player salaries. If Lynn doesn't want to jump off the bandwagon of this season's run for the Black and Blue Division's championship race, we can give the job to Prince Andrew and make him earn his regal salary.

Participants in the Bears-Cowboys game report that the fans didn't seem to know what was going on. "They didn't know when to cheer or not, but they seemed to be having a good time," the Refrigerator said.

That's the key for sports fans, anyway, having a good time. Fans can do the wave, eat three-dollar hotdogs, and wear Jim McMahon-style headbands and sunglasses whether the action is happening in a soccer stadium in jolly old England or in Bangladesh.

According to USA Today, NFL football is England's fastest growing spectator sport with almost four million tuning into televised regular season games, giving English wives a new definition of the old term "keeping a stiff upper lip," while they are ignored by their mates.

It's time to pressure the USFL to get on the stick and move to England before the NFL seizes all the wave lengths with Sunday football, Friday Night Football, and Saturday afternoon NFL action as well.

With no royal weddings on tap, and, knock on wood, no coronations, things look to be mighty dull next year for the British. Since they don't know much about football over there, they might think the USFL is a superior product because, to the Brits, duller is better. George Allen is just the man to pull the British away from their dart boards and reruns of *The Forsythe Saga*.

Football Terms as understood by Most British

Budweiser – a weak American beer delivered by horse and wagon.

Down lineman – too much action in the pub after the game.

Field goal – 100 bushels of maize per acre.

End zone – featured in the ads for 501 jeans.

Forward pass – an advance made toward a gentleman by a women's libber.

Goal line – misspelled version of Gaol Line, a prison wall.

Hail Mary pass – improper advance made in church.

Halfback – not enough stiff upper lip to be a fullback.

In the pocket – the little woman needs grocery money.

Linebacker – was late getting to the job office.

Prevent defense – an attempt to keep the population down.

Quarterback – less than a half back.

Red dog – an inferior hunting dog, too easily mistaken for the fox.

Rushing the quarterback – trying to get him to join the Goodfellows London Social Club.

Scrambling – one way to prepare eggs.

Special teams – groups organized to compete in such specialized events as steeplechasing.

Touchdown – catch 40 winks, visit the Land of Nod, hit the pillows.

Statue of Liberty play – an attempt by the Americans to ruin traditional English values by the importation of football.

Chapter 26
My deer hunting excuse

For every excuse to skip deer hunting, there's an all-American answer:

E: "I don't believe in killing; I support gun control."

A: When guns are outlawed, only outlaws will have guns.

E: "I don't shoot Walt Disney characters."

A: Take a good look at the wicked witch in *Snow White*.

E. "I don't like to fight the traffic up north."

A: Call in sick three days early.

E: "I don't hear so well anymore."

A: Shoot only what you can see.

E: "I can't see."

A: Stay in camp and cook. Familiarize yourself with the smell of pepper, garlic, chili powder, and Jim Beam.

E: "Nobody will hunt with me."

A: Take a bath. Try brushing your teeth once.

E: "I want to hit the bars opening weekend to flirt with the deer hunting widows."

A: Their men won't fire all the ammo during the hunt.

E: "I can't afford a license."

A: As the government said during the Vietnam war, if the economy can't afford both guns and butter, let it be guns.

E: "Last year I had buck fever and missed my deer."

A: Forget buck euchre, play five card draw.

E: "Last year I lost of my money playing poker."

A: Learn from your mistakes. Bring more money this year.

E: "I'm afraid of getting shot."

A: What makes you so special?

E: "I have to stay home and build a garage."

A: What are you, some kind of wimp?

People ask me why I don't hunt anymore. Well, I don't like to lie. The last time I hunted I was stationed at the head of a long point extending from the southwest corner of a 700-acre tamarack swamp. My mission was to secure this position against deer attacks while an army of insurgents swept through the tangle. I was responsible for that point and the area around the corner to the right.

I hadn't been on guard more than 15 minutes when a huge buck with trophy antlers attempted to sneak out the side of the swamp. Moving around the point, I shouldered the borrowed Long Tom and sighted in on the deer, which looked resentful. A gnat flew into my eye as I fired. The buck leaped a woven-wire fence and crossed into the neighboring woods.

I scarcely had time to reload the single shot before a large doe emerged from the same spot where the buck had shown himself. A dalliance? I wondered. The gunsight was dirty. My shot chased the doe over the fence.

Then three fawns came out of the swamp, in a single file. I had time to fire at each one before they learned of man's treachery and fled to sanctuary.

Deer hunting is really easy, I decided. Here I was, not even out an hour, and I already had scared five deer. But the fun was soon over. I saw nothing for the next hour. Finally, the Red Berets came out of the swamp.

"How many deer you got? Man, it sounded like the Tet Offensive."

"I didn't get a shot off. Those guys in the south woods must be having a field day, though. They must have got a crack at five, at least."

Why don't I go deer hunting? I don't like to lie.

Chapter 27

Is Betty Crocker a man?

It's a mystery why companies pay up to a quarter of a million bucks for three squiggly lines that a designer calls a "logo." Sure, the logo expert can explain what these lines mean. "Notice the little hook at the bottom of the left line. That's to get the consumer's last dollar. The center line, that stands for the main man, the guy at the top who turns all the wheels. That line on the right, well, this is a conservative company."

After large bags of gold transfer from a Fortune 500 company to the designer, the public doesn't know what the symbol means or even what company it stands for, unless the company name is printed in huge letters alongside of the logo. What a joke! The consumer never goes on a blind date with a logo.

Showcasing corporate identity can be lots simpler. Look what General Mills did with Betty Crocker. Her name and picture are known everywhere. She gets thousands of letters every month asking questions ranging from how to get Junior away from the television set to how to bake an angel food cake at the North Pole. Though she's 65, she gets marriage proposals all the time, many from men young enough to be her grandsons.

I first proposed to Betty through the mail in 1955, when her picture was redrawn to give her a more friendly image. Things weren't going well in my romantic life at the time. Within a week I'd been jilted by two of my girlfriends, a redheaded Belgian from Milroy and a petite brunette

Norwegian from Belview.

Betty was a mature lady at the time, 34. I was a teenager, but I ate a lot of cake. I knew she wouldn't string a guy along for a while and then drop him for the football quarterback or the only son of a rich farmer with 360 acres of level, black soil.

"I love your picture," I wrote. "I'm glad you don't have those pursed lips anymore. You used to look like you'd put too much alum in the garlic dills. Could I please have an autographed picture and a free box of chocolate crumb cake?" I passed the waiting days by listening to Fats Domino records and putting dimes in pinball machines.

Weeks passed before I received a letter from Betty's boss. "Thank you for your interest in our corporate symbol. Since the redesigning of her picture, Betty has received literally dozens and dozens of marriage proposals from all over the globe – a powerful testimony to the viability of this symbol. Betty regrets that she cannot accept all these offers of matrimony, but she is a career gal. In appreciation, however, she is sending you this eight by ten glossy of a box of our newest cake mix, Pineapple Orange Delite, also five cents off coupon."

Though disappointed I went to the store and bought the box of cake. I ate the whole thing warm from the oven. I had been thwarted in my romantic tendencies, but Betty remained in my heart as the Grail I would seek in my life's quest. Cake would be the symbol of my pursuit of excellence.

Ten years later I was married. The doctor ordered me to lay off sweets. One Friday afternoon while taking a secret stroll down the cake mix aisle, I stopped in my tracks, my attention riveted to a display ad featuring Betty's picture. Feeling shock, horror, and disbelief, I realized that Betty's picture had been redrawn. She now looked like Jackie Kennedy.

I could care less about Jackie. I was secretly in love with Ladybird Johnson, who had addressed me as "sugah" in Mankato during the 1960 Presidential campaign. I lost all romantic interest in Betty.

Since that time Betty has had face lifts, tummy tucks, and new hair engineering in 1968, 1972, and 1980. I warmed up a little to the 1968 picture, which made Betty look like a cross between Mary Tyler Moore and Charlotte Bronte, but by the time Betty was redesigned in 1972 – this time looking like Ladybird – I didn't care. I had a crush on Farah Fawcet.

Betty's most recent changeover has just been announced. She doesn't look a day over 53, with her dress-for-success suit and hoop earrings. Her face exudes confidence, coolness, frankness, the kind of countenance that could sell furnaces in Cairo. An Associated Press article describes her as a middle-age yuppie.

The new Betty works 60 hours a week, bakes her cakes in a microwave, and breakfasts on toaster pastries and caffeine-free coffee. She and her husband work in separate cities and fly together for the weekends. The company expects a few marriage proposals. I sent the following letter:

Dear Betty:

> *You might remember my marriage proposal from 1955, also my letter objecting to your face in 1965. Now that I am happily married I cannot ask for your hand. I would consider an open-type relationship in which you share me with your financial patronage in support of my writing career. Since I saw your new picture, I can't get you out of my mind. I can't believe the change since you first pursed your lips in 1936. You look so much more desirable with the grey gone from your hair. I wish I knew your secret of getting younger every few years, as it takes me several hours and ten cups of coffee to unthaw my arthritic joints every morning. By the way, if you change your image again soon, study some pictures of Madonna and Cindy Lauper.*

Romantically inclined,

Don

> *P.S. I know you don't go on blind dates. To get to know me better, meet me June 12 at noon in Abdul's Pita Palace.*

A few days ago I narrowly avoided getting beaten up in a fist fight with a redneck who told me that Betty is actually a man. I considered defending her honor but decided instead to outrun him. When I got home, I called the company to verify Betty's femininity.

The spokesman told me: "Betty was born in 1921 as the pen name of a male company employee who figured housewives would have more confidence if they thought a woman was answering their inquiries. The prim look suggests that she never has an accident in the kitchen, just as the housewife who uses our products will always achieve culinary success."

"Are you still there?" the company official asked. I was there. I just couldn't talk. All these years I had carried a torch for – and proposed to – a Man! Never again would I trust outward appearances. The federal government should mandate an Olympic-style sex test for all corporate symbols and logos.

Chapter 28
Polite to a fault

Minnesotans love foreigners. Never was that folk trait so apparent as during the 1987 World Series. With open arms we embraced – no, we have to close our arms to embrace – news and sports reporters and baseball fans from Missouri, South Dakota, Illinois, California, and even the exotic Far East, Manhattan.

These visitors reacted with relief, surprise, and despair. Baseball writers accustomed to walking with their heads crooked halfway behind them returned to their urban newspapers relieved that they tested mug-free. Surprised they had been invited to share taxi rides with Nordic strangers. Despairing because there were no overturned cars and burning store fronts to provide an angle to the post-game victory celebrations.

If they had been properly briefed before coming to walleye land, they would have learned Minnesotans are polite – to a fault.

As cars pass each other on the freeways at 70 mph, occupants stare politely at each other, wondering who has the best garden.

Drivers yield to pedestrians in the crosswalks, scarcely cursing the fools who crash into their rear ends when they make those sudden courtesy stops. Pedestrians wave "go ahead" to the approaching traffic, willing to wait all day if necessary for that rare moment when the cars stop coming.

At salad bars we furtively ladle the olive that has bounced off our heaped-up plate and fallen into the blue cheese dressing.

When someone in the video store jealously eyes *Revenge of the Nerds: Part X* – our evening's cultural plan – we say, "Go ahead. You take it. I'm too bushed to watch TV tonight."

We don't stare very long at attractive ladies getting out of their cars while wearing miniskirts.

At the school parent conferences we sit politely while Miss Murdstone tells us "Joshua certainly has a lot of energy" or "Nicole really takes a mature attitude toward boys."

Farmers driving along a county road wave at every oncoming car, even though it may be harboring a feed salesman or a candidate for President of the United states.

We feel guilty when telephone salespeople call up. Even though we don't have three hours to waste listening to a vacuum cleaner sales pitch, we agree to a free carpet shampooing because that vigorous young salesman might be a struggling college student who needs big profits to maintain his social life.

In the supermarket checkout line, we pull aside our heaping carts in favor of the bachelor who is in a hurry to get home to prepare his evening meal of canned sardines and salsa.

We covet – but don't steal from – our neighbor's woodpiles.

We covet – but only when he isn't home – our neighbor's wife.

We keep our fish houses at least two feet apart.

As a jogger gets within a half block, we move aside to avoid a collision. The athlete moves aside. We move again. The jogger moves again. Checkmate!

We feel guilty as we take the last sheet of toilet paper off the roll without intending to replace it.

College students blow their noses on toilet paper because there's no room in their bookbags or jeans pockets for even a travel pack of tissue. So the janitors usually put a few rolls on the book shelves in the lavatories. One day, while suffering an extreme case of the "college crud," that dread disease that causes constant coughing and runny noses, I entered the lav, only to find no rolls on the shelf.

I entered a stall. No paper. The holder was gone too. The second stall had also been robbed. In the third stall the holder was gone, but a new roll had been invitingly placed on the floor. I picked it up, intending to carry it to my office. Then Minnesota pride set in. I put the roll down and returned to grade essays, mucus dripping into my mustache.

Most surprising of all to aliens is our behavior at sporting events. We stand up at basketball games for the other team's fight song, even though we hate the next town and everything it represents.

At amateur baseball games, our worst heckling consists of yelling at a struggling pitcher. "Stick a fork in him, he's done."

During the American League playoffs, we got angry at Juan Berenguer for showing enthusiasm, worried that the opponents might become embarrassed and not like us.

At the end of the World Series we told Cardinal fans, "Yeah, you guys had a good team. We were lucky to win it. Maybe another time you'd beat us if you tried harder."

When it comes to politeness, as Tom Wolfe would say, Minnesotans have "The Right Stuff."

Chapter 29

The ghost of Halloween past

"Villie" Schlesinger's ghost appeared to me about the first of October this year. His wiggling pipe reproached me, reminding me of the only time in my life when I did the wrong thing.

As teenagers growing up in a town smaller than Mayberry, we took our meager pleasures when and where we could. More than anything else, we got a kick out of picking on the old "moostaches," who to a man showed no interest in important cultural vestiges like football, baseball, apple pie, and the English language. "Villie," a Pomeranian immigrant who lived next door to my grandfather, was the perfect target.

Those were the golden days when a man's outhouse was a home away from home, a last refuge from the high costs of hooking up to the village sanitary system and the unsanitary conditions of indoor plumbing. Each Halloween "Villie's" outhouse was the first to go down, as he screamed Teutonic curses at the departing Al Capones.

The year came when I was judged mature enough to vandalize. We spent the early hours of the evening ransacking gardens for ripe cucumbers and decaying beets to hurl at the wily North Korean and Red Chinese soldiers we imagined lurking behind every spirea bush. Little children's trick or treat bags succumbed to armed robbery.

An hour before the curfew tolled "the knell of parting day," we advanced through the alley toward the Schlesinger castle. "Holy balls, he's out there!" Schimmel(1) yelled. We hit the dirt in my grandfathers' garden, rotting tomatoes squishing into our shirt fronts. I raised my head and took a peek. "It's his scarecrow," I said. We ran to the outhouse and hid behind it.

Lacking a chain and four-wheel drive pickup, we put our shoulders to the task. Nothing happened. "Let's try it again," Goose(2) said. It didn't budge. "Everybody push, hard," Duke(3) said, showing the kind of leadership destined to lift him to prison or the Presidency. "It's gotta go." One mighty heave – Hernia City. It stood proud.

Just then the police car, Constable Smith at the wheel, pulled into the alley. We took off running. I ran all the way home, so fast I had time hear most of *Lux Radio Theatre*. "What happened to your shirt?" my mother asked.

"Tomato fight."

The next day after school we returned to the scene of the attempted crime and examined the outhouse. This ignorant foreigner had braced each corner with four by fours sunk into the ground. Nothing less than a Sherman tank would have rocked it. As we stood staring at each other, "Villie" came out of the house, his mustache dripping with tobacco, and wiggled his pipe at us. We waved back and took off running. Next Halloween we would tackle an easier project – blowing up the state bank.

Notes:

(1) German for "white horse," the nickname in those days for one of the rarest types in that town: a blonde boy.

(2) Nickname for anybody in the school who couldn't pronounce "alunium."

(3) As the military says, better a bad leader than no leader.

Chapter 30

Educational bankruptcy

The nations' governors have issued a report recommending an educational bankruptcy system that would allow states to seize control of school districts that fail to achieve minimum learning standards. A typical scenario might look like this...

Superintendent Millard Cooledge

Hog Wallow District No. 60

Hog Wallow, ...

Dear Superintendent:

During the past academic year, results from the eighth grade math proficiency tests show that your district finished in the bottom one percent of all state schools. Your results on the reading proficiency exams were barely measurable. In addition, 22 percent of your seniors failed to qualify for a regular diploma due to failing required minimum competency exams.

As a consequence, the State Board of Education has declared your district to be in educational bankruptcy and is foreclosing on all your assets. Mr. Wyatt E. Rup has been appointed receiver. Please welcome him and consider any of his requests as orders from the State Board.

Yours educationally,

Randall P. Shoe

Executive Director,

State Board of Education

Superintendent Cooledge hastily convenes a special school board meeting. "As you recall, I've been asking for that special mill levy for years," he tells the board. "Now we're in the soup."

Board members are outraged. "They can't do this to us. We're debt free," comments Calabash. Comments of chairman Keynard Fox are unprintable.

Cooledge lets them stew a while, then he says, "I have prepared a rebuttal. I would like your authorization to send this list of district assets to the state board to prove that we are in educational solvency,"

ASSETS:

One multi-purpose educational building. The original building constructed in 1898, an addition completed in 1952, a final addition in 1961. The last bonds paid off in 1981. Note: we are debt free.

One gala athletic complex completed in 1978: Football field. All-weather track. Three practice football fields. Lighted softball field. School district golf course. Six gyms for wrestling, basketball, volleyball, and aerobics.

A three-year football won loss record of 26-6 (should have been 27-5 except for that lousy clipping call in the General Stonewall Jackson game).

Boys' basketball teams in the state tournament five times in nine years. Girls' state runner-up last year.

Tennis champions, double and singles, in 1980, 1982, and 1983-89.

Twenty-two of last year's graduates received partial or full scholarships for college athletics.

Baseball district champions three times in last eight years.

Tallest corn in any FFA test plot in the state.

Eighty percent of our teachers below the age of 29.

Senior Amy Grosstart won Best Dressed Senior in the State from the Fashion Council.

Sixty-two percent of juniors and seniors attended last year's prom. Twenty-four percent of sophomores, an outstanding total since they had to be asked by an upperclassman.

Smoke-free environment in the building due to establishment of the Roger Twitchell Memorial Smoking area by the back parking lot entrance to the metal shop.

Largest auto mechanic shop in the state.

Development of the "I'm the cheese" program to enhance student self-images.

Two hundred thirty-one trees planted on school ground last year alone. Total trees planted over 500 in three years.

Judd Dawkins up there in typing was one of the top 25 finalists for State Teacher of the Year.

"I could list assets. However, this list should prove to the state boys that we are in no way bankrupt."

"Excuse me," interrupts Acacia Fillbert, the board's token woman. "You're always forgetting our girls. You'd better put down that trophy case full of Future Homemaker awards."

"Very apt point, Acacia. I'll make a note of that. Yes, this list shows that we're in excellent shape. Oh, we can do a few things to clean up our act. For example, the wrestling program is really sick. And just because we're a Southern state is no excuse that we don't have a hockey team. We've got to get that ice arena built. We can't start a team and expect our kids to drive all the way to Memphis for practice."

"Well I must agree," Fox says, "except for the hockey part. That would take away from our already watered-down wrestling program. When I won State at 119 in '48..."

"Forget ancient history," says Calabash. "We need a winner now, in every sport. I move to fire Coach Russell right now. That should shut up the state in a hurry."

Cooledge adds, "Normally I wouldn't support firing a coach because of his won and loss record, but the State Board is carrying a 20-ounce hammer. They want better school performance, and they want it now."

Member Robert E. Jefferson Davis Lee has been silent up to this point. "Let's all remember the State Board isn't as concerned about all these athletic achievements as we are. They basically want improved skills in the three R's. We have to show them good faith in the academic areas too."

Cooledge and the board members sit and state at each other for a little while. It is so quiet you can hear a pecan drop. Then Fox speaks up.

"Here it is. We'll get a computer for every kid. That oughta keep the chalk out of the pawn shop."

Chapter 31
Deer hunting on the homefront

It's not Bolshevik Russia in 1919. The beards don't cover up contagious skin diseases. The town has not been invaded by an obscure religious cult. Sales of schnapps, blackberry brandy, and case beer go up 150 percent. Small groups of men meander sheepishly through the supermarket buying eggs and bacon, beans and smelly cheese. Women slave overtime in hot kitchens making huge quantities of stew and chili.

Streets fill with four-wheel-drive vehicles of every make, vintage, and color. The battle of Iwo-Jima is re-enacted at the gun range. The .30-.30 replaces the four-foot level in pickup rear windows. Cartridge belts replace seat belts. It's the Minnesota deer opener.

As fast as they appeared, the four-wheelers head out of town. Decrepit green and blue school buses topped with television dishes roll down the highways, headed north. Lights are extinguished in the workshops of the vast Big Shed Country. Essential services close down as barbers, hardware merchants, plumbers, bankers, and psychologists leave the city. Schools report a high rate of illness.

Grocery store shopping carts fill with convenience foods: boil in a bag fillet mignon, TV dinners, gourmet frozen macaroni and cheese. Shopping centers teem with smiling women and heated up credit cards. The only men in the discount stores are over 70, look like wimps, or disguise themselves in orange Jones hats and laminated hooded sweatshirts.

Formerly bored housewives bounce with new life. They graze in packs in all the area restaurants. The few men remaining in town slouch around, peeking furtively around the corners. Church message boards advertise the Sunday sermon: "What to do if your man is killed in the woods." Attendance at services doubles. Deer hunter wives review the insurance policies.

The Big Lie rides into town in campers and buses; the hunt is over for another year. It was too cold – the gun froze up just as I sighted in on a 14-pointer. There wasn't enough snow for tracking. The deer weren't moving. They were in the swamps where we couldn't get at them without a duck boat. Our group wasn't big enough to drive them. We didn't have doe permits. I don't shoot yearlings. A whole herd moved in on us, but then the wind changed. Most of our group is getting too old to make the tough shots. I don't care if I get a deer or not; I just like to go with the boys out to the woods. The Indians have cleaned them all out where we hunted. The wolves have cleaned them all out where we hunted. The bow hunters have cleaned them all out where we hunted.

Reality has been left behind in the deer camp with the cigar butts, the empty shells, and the beer cheese rinds. Hunters take out home improvement loans to cover their poker losses. Missed shots double in range and difficulty. The lucky guy who was barely missed by somebody's "sound" shot vows to give up the chase.

Gutless passengers ride unwillingly on the tops and trunk lids of cars. A purple school bus heads down Main Street with 12 corpses on top. A real school bus driver stares at it in amazement. How many times he has wished he could gut out his junior high pupils and throw them on top of the bus!

The men return home. Their wives count the hunter's fingers and toes. They pull out the charge slips and start planning the next week's menus. Arguments break out over who spent the most money – the deer hunter or the war widow who stayed home.

To some degree most of us have survived another deer hunting season in Minnesota. The casualty rate for the deer is 25 percent, slightly lower than the casualty rate for the hunters' marriages.

Chapter 32

Let's talk turkey

In 1988, courtesy of a First District farmer, President Ronald Reagan was presented with a Minnesota-grown turkey for Thanksgiving. Early the next spring I had the opportunity to interview this 50-pounder, Benjamin, who hadn't fared as well as Wilfred, the 1987 White House meal.

When I arrived at his southern Minnesota farm, Benjamin was standing placidly atop a turkey shed. "I'm surprised to see you here alive and back on the farm," I said. "Usually all that's left of the President's official turkey by this time is the heartburn from too much ala king."

"That's true, unfortunately. I would have been better off dead, than living now with all the bad memories."

"Tell me your story."

"It was a cold day in Washington when I arrived in a crate at the White House. I was looking forward to my demise after overdosing on Jerry Clower tapes all the way from Minnesota in an 18-wheeler. In fact, I accepted my fate gladly. I had thought back to Reagan's First Inaugural Address in 1981, when he asked Americans to all share in the cost of his *new beginning.*

"I was prepared to rest my head and fate on the woodchopper's block, the President himself delivering the *coup de grace.* Let there be no misunderstanding. Any of us is better off dead and stuffed with bread than Red.

"But Washington is a place of secret intrigues. People bustle around doing things that have no names. Only Congress writes checks. In weeks, graduates of secretarial schools rise from stenographer to Assistant Director of the CIA. Senate pages turn warlord.

"Before I even got out of the crate, I was spirited out of the White House, transported by taxi to an airport, and loaded in the cargo hold of a gigantic airplane. The plane took off before I could ask where we were going. That's an existential question anyway. Who among us knows where we are going or when, or why, or even why we are here at all?

"After many hours the plane landed in an alien place that looked like Miami Beach with Hebrew signs. Part of the cargo was unloaded. I remained in the plane, unfed and unwatered.

"After many hours of flying, marked by the kind of air turbulence that indicates that we were flying over mountains, we landed once again. Our crates stayed in heaps for quite a few hours. Dozing off, I was awakened by the call to the mosque.

"When the prayer hour was completed, we were loaded into military trucks, and our caravan started out. As we climbed up some hills, I recognized familiar scenes that took me all the way back to Mrs. Murdstone's eighth grade geography class. We were leaving Pakistan. I would soon be celebrating Thanksgiving with Afghan rebels. I would be sacrificing to fight communism after all. I settled down for a nap."

"How did you escape this fate that's worse than the fate that's worse than death?" I asked.

"It's a simple story really. We were transported by donkey caravan to a rebel camp. The ground was dotted with hundreds and hundreds of supply crates, mostly filled with various weapons, ammo, and spare military parts; but some contained American GI combat rations – stuff like dried fruit and peanut butter. I was nestled between a crate of dried salad dressing and a crate of dehydrated White Castles – with cheese.

"The Afghanis picked up the military supplies and hauled them away. Then they glanced at the food crates. An authoritative figure who looked like an emaciated Clint Eastwood tossed around a few packs of rations.

"The rebels looked bored. They opened up a few of the cartons, dipped their fingers in the peanut butter, tasted it, and spit it out. Several Afghanis attempted to chew the dried apricots. I screamed at them. "Try the peanut butter on bread. Put a little goat cheese in your sandwich. Jelly, too, if you have some. And the fruit, soak it in water!' But my gobbles fell on un-American ears.

"A day passed. Along with the other leftovers I returned to Pakistan. Either they didn't see me amidst all the peanut butter, or they thought I was some kind of American pig. Soon I was in another airplane, heading for parts unknown.

"I won't bore you with the despicable tortures I suffered in Iran at the hands of Khomeini's right hand man, the spy trial that two crates of dried apples and I endured in Iraq, or the drudgery of waiting in line at a bank in the Grand Caymans while the pilot deposited a few millions destined for anonymous Swiss bank accounts.

"Nor will I detail the intestinal disorder I suffered in Camp Contra in Honduras. By this time I had developed an extreme case of inferiority. Didn't foreigners like turkey, I wondered or did they consider me an ugly American? After a few skirmishes inside Nicaragua, I was shipped back to the states and once again deposited in the White House back yard.

"I called my congressman, Tim Penny, to ask him what the deal was. He said, 'For security reasons the President cannot accept gifts of food. You will be placed in the Washington Zoo's petting ground.'

"I asked him, 'You mean in a bistro, the Senate offices, the Wilbur Memorial Fountain, or where?'

"It turned out to be an actual zoo. If you think congressmen are terrible people, you ought to meet their kids. In two days I was climbing the walls. Give me the Ayatollah any time."

"But you finally escaped?"

"I talked turkey to Rudy Boschwitz. He needed a diversion from the current arms shipment scandal – I call it – Gobblegate – so he flew me back to Minnesota and put me to work. He said, 'There are too many turkeys in Washington already.' You'll see me on TV soon. I've filmed some ads with his boys. I'm the best darned wallpaper salesman you've ever seen.

Chapter 33
If it's free, take it

"If it's free, take it," a wise friend once told me. Although his advice came too late for me to capitalize on the antique craze, I still managed to fill up my garage with telephone insulators, blue Mason jars, West Albion creamery cans, stove pipe, lumber scraps, and broken cement blocks. My craze for collecting finally came to an end, however, the day my hobby narrowly missed demolishing my neighbor's house.

For a long time I had coveted one of those big spools that hold wire. I pictured one, painted a redwood color, dominating the patio at my lake cabin. I could see the beads of sweat forming on the iced tea pitcher.

When the telephone company began laying the underground wire, the golden opportunity had come. As I drove along a country road, I saw a whole row of empty spools spaced at intervals. Since "procrastination is the thief of time," I stopped along the road and attracted the attention of the operator of a giant backhoe. When I asked what the plans were for the spools, he said, "Take one. Get a pickup or trailer and I'll load it for you."

The true scrounger always worries that someone else will get there ahead of him. I hurried to town and borrowed a trailer. Remember, if you always borrow a trailer, you don't have to buy a license. I rushed back where angels fear to tread.

After the equipment operator had loaded the spool into the low-sided trailer, he asked if I had some rope or chain to tie it down with. "No," I replied confidently. "It's heavy enough to stay in place. It'll never go anywhere."

Our cabin was situated on a steep hill overlooking beautiful Lake Sylvia.

The access road that rose steeply from the bottom of the hill where two cabins were situated resembled a goat path. Although it was wide enough for a car or small truck, the main track was two eroded ruts. Getting to the top required fast acceleration and driving agility, if not foolhardy recklessness.

Halfway up the hill, the car spun out from the weight of the spool on the trailer. I carefully backed down to get another run. Reaching the bottom of the hill, I paused for a minute of self-congratulation for the skillful job of backing. I gunned the car and headed up the hill.

As I got to the spot where I stalled out before, this time with considerably more speed, the trailer fishtailed, one wheel skidded into the rut I was carefully avoiding, and the spool bounced off the trailer, headed down the hill.

It's funny how our first thoughts at the time of tragedy can be about insignificant things. As a person falls out of the boat, he thinks, "If I drown, I'll miss part two of that *A Team* rerun." My first thoughts on this occasion were about devious ways to sucker six people into coming out here to help me reload the spool.

The spool bounced down the hill with the rough rhythm of an unbalanced tire – two revolutions, thump-bump, a crooked veer. Then it straightened itself. When it hit a larger rock, it wobbled, started sideways, and then corrected its roll.

At that moment I became conscious of the two cabins at the bottom of the hill. Like nuclear fission, my mind fragmented into multiple personalities. The rational WASP was still concerned with reloading the spool. A housewife bent down to remove a panful of cookies from the oven just as the giant spool crashed through the wall as though it were cardboard. Then I saw myself as an experienced liar trying to explain the mishap to my insurance company.

The spool continued its bouncing meander. With relief, I saw that the first cabin was set back far enough from the road to be out of danger. The last cabin was the threatened one.

Another personality emerged into consciousness. This time I was the proud husband and father, coming home after a hard days work, only to see his home destroyed by the rampant spool, his wife dead, cookies scattered all over the kitchen.

At this point the spool hit another rock and skipped to the right, headed harmlessly toward the woods. My heart was full. Then the spool righted itself and continued its inexorable roll. Almost at the bottom of the hill the spool bounced left and headed right for the cabin. One of my personalities stared through the bars in a futile search for a hacksaw.

At the last second the spool corrected its bounce and veered right again, headed for the neighbor's fish house at 40 miles an hour. It hit the shack like a game warden intent on catching somebody inside with extra lines down. The spool lodged in the crushed walls.

Life is full of little decisions. My first impulse was to take it on the lam since no one had come out of the cabin to see if a plane had crashed nearby. If I left in a hurry, nobody would ever know the trouble I had seen. But I was worried about the ruined shack. After all, in Minnesota, "A man's fish house is his castle."

Then five hundred years of Protestant morality intruded its bearded head. I left my name and phone number on a slip of paper and went to town, wondering how I could ever atone for the grievous harm. When I returned that evening with my insurance information, the neighbor was reconciled to the fate of his fish house. He said he would take the insurance settlement and build a new one, "a four-holer this time."

Despite the amicable ending to the incident, I determined to stop the scrounging habit. That next winter, though, was the year of the big snow, dozens of fish house floors had been abandoned on the ice of area lakes. As a patriotic citizen, I began to remove them. Maybe they would come in handy someday.

Chapter 34

Requiem for an ice dog

Anybody but the DNR and a few commonsense freaks will say that the time to get out for the best ice fishing is when the ice first forms. If there is no snow cover, two inches of ice might feel rubbery but is generally strong enough to support a person walking. The problem is knowing how to safely test the ice.

Over the years we have found that the best method is to send a dog ahead, because most dogs are good enough swimmers to scramble out of the water and swim to shore if they break through. We've had a number of scout dogs over the years, some good, some bad. Lad, a beautiful red setter, failed his first summer training session when he refused to swim. We lost our Doberpoodle, Klink, because he didn't swim. A good swimmer, Rex was afraid of thin ice but was an expert at gaffing walleyes with the hook we attached in place of the paw he lost in a trap. Then we got the best one we ever had.

I'll never forget him, my old dog Tray, a combination black lab and schnauzer. Tray went from beginning swimming through advanced life saving in just two lessons at the beach. Swimming is only half of it, though. We had to find out if he was combat ready.

One night in late October we took Tray down to the hockey rink, shortly after the hockey association had flooded it for the first time. Millions of stars twinkled in the clear, frosty air like schools of Mille Lacs walleyes. Tray strained against his collar, chain taut. With a final pat on the flank, I released the chain from the collar and called out, "Go, Tray. Check the ice!" Tray started with a leap and dashed the length of the rink like a puck destined for an icing call. When he got to the other end, he turned around and roared back without even glancing at the warming house. We were so excited by Tray's *elan* that we left for home without even drilling any holes.

In early November Tray started going out on his own, testing pond ice. By Thanksgiving, our traditional opener, he was in shape to test the bays on Clearwater Lake. Well, he was every bit as good as his promise. Sometimes we caught fish, sometimes we got skunked, but Tray was consistent all that season and in years to come. He would sit nervously at the back of the 1969 Ford ice fishing car by the wood burning stove, head bobbing up and down, long tongue licking an imaginary crappie. When he arrived at the lake shore, Tray would bound eagerly onto the ice, at least in his salad years (When he was young and had good digestion, he liked a little lettuce with his beer batter-fried fish). Toward the end of his career, though, he got more and more reluctant to step on the ice. We knew he was washed up the year he refused to leave the car. We were on our own again, depending on chisel to test the ice. Tray must have known that he had failed us, because he passed away that winter, his spirit broken.

The next spring we got a new pup, a great Dane-dachshund-lab merger. Toivo came from a long line of West Albion ice testers. The first time we took him out to a frozen pond in the fall, he charged exuberantly onto the ice, as we rubbed our hands with glee. Suddenly, he started to break through the ice, but with a windmill motion, he climbed back on the ice shelf and raced to shore, feet barely touching the ice. The smell of wood smoke beckoned him to the car's hospitable warmth. We knew Toivo was as ready as good genes and careful training could make him.

Shortly after this first test, Toivo disappeared for about a week. Unfortunately, this was one of those sporadic times when Annandale had a dog catcher. The call came. "We are holding your dog Toivo. You can ransom him for twenty-five dollars in costs and boarding fees." Chuckling to ourselves, we made arrangements to pick him up. If only the city had known Toivo's real worth!

About two weeks after his commencement exercises, we headed out to Kewpees's for the opener. By the time we had walked to the shoreline with our equipment, Toivo was already on the edge of the ice, but *weltschmertz* darkened his features. We were prepared for this kind of emergency, however, and threw a couple of sirloin steaks about thirty feet ahead of him on the ice. Toivo went for the gusto. We started out slowly behind him, the ice cracking like an old wooden floor. The noise drove him off in a panic. Well, we knew we were smarter than a dog and probed our way out to the fishing spot. We gently chopped holes in the inch and a half ice and dropped our lines in.

In spite of Toivo's disgrace, it was a beautiful day out – cold, calm air, the whistling of a late flight of goldeneyes, the smell of basswood smoke from the car parked at the boat landing, Toivo scratching at the car door. Unfortunately, the fish did not seem to be there. We tried waxworms, goldenrods, angleworms, cream-style corn. We used Fairy Jigs, Mitzi Ditzis, Moon Glows, Flutter Chucks, Doctor Spoons, every shape and color in our extensive repertoire assembled from Little Jim's Bait Shop. Finally we wrapped our lines and threaded our way carefully back to the car. Toivo greeted us enthusiastically, but the feeling was not mutual.

It was a grim trip to the St. Cloud Humane Society. Once when I leaned back to put a piece of wood in the stove, Toivo tentatively licked my hand, but I drove onward, unrelenting. Even the prospect of bargains next door at Gopher Lumber did not divert me from my adoption center. The smell of animal pens matched my mood. "Give Toivo a good home," I told the lady behind the counter, "but don't give him to an ice fisherman."

We go out on our own now. We still like dogs, but we haven't been able to find one to replace old Tray in our hearts and on the ice. For those of you who might like to try a seeing-ice dog, one word of warning: if the dog starts to break through the ice, proceed ahead to the fishing spot with great caution.

Chapter 35

The care and feeding of husbands

An article in a women's magazine promised to reveal "50 Special Ways to Show You Love Your Lover." The list was the usual stuff: bake him a cake, listen to his political opinions without yawning, trim his hair, wear black lace things, write "I Love You" on the bathroom mirror, take a massage class, laugh at his jokes, give him a gift certificate for hang gliding.

These lists are always written by women who think they know what men want. Those magazines should ask men what they want. Then a typical list on "The Care and Feeding of Husbands" would read something like this...

1. Men really get turned on by the smell of gasoline exhaust. Mow the lawn in summer and run the snow blower in winter. In the off season you can till up the garden. He will usually come out and watch.

2. Learn taxidermy to help him preserve his favorite memories. This could develop into a lucrative part-time job for you, while he spends his spare time in the outdoors.

3. Perform all the routine maintenance on the family vehicles. Women look cute with grease under their fingernails. While you're at it, throw in a new set of spark plugs.

4. Attend a baseball or football game with him and pretend to be enjoying yourself. Be the person to lead "The Wave" in your section of the grandstand.

5. Always clean the fish. Men are tired when they get home after a day on the lake and need to unwind with a bottle of beer and cable movie.

6. Don't offer to go deer hunting with the men. Absence makes the heart grow fonder. The woods are too rugged for women. At least the card games are.

7. When he's watching television and ignoring you, rub taco chips on your face and hands and snuggle up to him.

8. Bring your knitting on a night out at the neighborhood tavern so you aren't bored while he is playing video poker.

9. Call attention to attractive females that he might miss seeing. While he is ogling, his mind will return to those thrilling days of yesteryear.

10. Practice preventive medicine. Men's romantic desires decline sharply when they are forced to carry out the garbage.

11. Remember that the car is an extension of the person. Always compliment his driving. "You're such a good driver you could even drive in New York City or St. Cloud!"

12. He'll really get turned on when he sees your reflection in the shoes you have just polished for him.

13. Destroy your charge cards.

14. Be available at all times to change television channels.

15. Pile up a nice stack of wood beside the front door and bring in a few pieces every time you go in the house.

16. Make a profit on your garage sales. Sell more than you buy at other people's sales.

17. Wear last year's clothes.

18. Wear buck scent.

To quote Kathryn Falk, editor of *Romantic Times*, "Most men are not romantic. But women are, and they should spend the time and energy to make romance happen, to teach their men what it's all about." Starting with this list of 18 suggestions, it should be easy for you ladies to think up equally imaginative ways "To Show You Love Your Lover." If you always keep his desires in the forefront, his interest in you is certain to increase.

Chapter 36
Ice fishing lies

Many people think that ice fishing is a convivial sport, a time to drink beer, smoke cigars, and exchange lies with your friends; but the fact is that true ice fishing is not a sport but a way of life, a life of pain, loneliness, disillusionment, and hard work – the origin of the saying, "It's a dirty job, but somebody has to do it."

If you want to catch fish, avoid the so called "hot spots." Those spots with thirty fishing shacks clustered so close together that the inmates can almost hook each other's lines are great places to socialize, but the fact is that constant noise will spook the fish and drive them to new places. For real success, you must find your own spots away from everyone else. You must become "The Lone Ice Fisherman."

The easiest way to be alone is to be the first one out on the thin ice at the beginning of winter. Of course, you may be risking your life, but Ernest Hemingway and other "death wish" philosophers would agree that the risk is well worth the chance of catching a pailful of sunfish or a big walleye. If you do venture out on thin ice, follow a few commonsense rules. Eat a small breakfast. Probe your way carefully with a chisel, retreating if you suddenly find the knuckles of your hand that is holding the chisel shaking hands with the ice surface. Leave your fish house at home. Wear an inner tube. Bring a weight to hold your pail down so it doesn't float away if the ice is so rubbery that water comes up out of the holes.

No matter how hard you strive for anonymity, you must prepare for visits from curious fishermen who will walk over to see what the heck you are doing in that spot anyway. One way to ensure privacy is to fish in a house so people can't see what you are doing. Be sure to immediately kill any fish with a ball peen hammer, lest the noise of the fish flopping in your pail or against the floor of the fish house gives you away to people fishing outside. If you are fishing in a new spot, bring a portable house along. Some people even put out a decoy house with their name on it and then fish on a different lake. If you have to fish outside, use an opaque pail with a cover on it and only a small hole through which to deposit your catch. Never get off your pail because somebody might come over and look in it. Besides if you walk away from your spot, you might become the victim of a hole jumper.

You can also use your clothing for an edge. One of the area's top fishermen wears a knee-length sheepskin coat, sits on his pail with his legs straddling the hole, and fishes between the folds of his coat. Unless you are looking directly at him from a distance of no more than three feet, you will never know he is catching fish.

Above all, if you are to become a successful ice fisherman, you must learn the greatest secret. You must learn to lie. The effectiveness of the lie as a fishing tool was pointed out to me years ago at the point of rushes out from Ann's Bait Shop. A solitary fisherman was jigging with that peculiar action known to fishermen and teenagers as "pimpling." He convincingly assured me there were no fish around. As I walked away my young son Eric said reverently, "Did you see the gigantic walleye head peeping through the opening at the top of his pail?" Most people who fish for sunfish work it the same way. Somebody with half a pail of big "sunnies" might admit to catching three or four little ones.

Some ice fishermen with a little more honor will resist the bald lie but will resort when necessary to evasion. One winter some of the top locals were bringing in pails of big sunfish from Clearwater. Numerous trips to the lake failed to reveal the secret spot. No one would tell me where they were catching fish because of the unwritten rule that states, "Ice fishermen must never reveal their sources." I finally humbled myself and asked one of these lucky and talented people where the fish were biting. "Clearwater," he answered without blinking an eye. I swallowed the last bite of crow and asked, "On the west side?" Feeling sorry for me, he confided, "Sort of."

Chapter 37
O come all ye faithful

Unlike most rites of passage, the Christmas Sunday School program measures life's progress in slow degrees. Starting in the front pew, where every wiggle attracts the pastor's attention, Jenny and Johnny move one row farther back each year, each time taking on a greater burden of verses to memorize, until, with the arrival of puberty, comes the responsibility to uphold the singing. To the small children, the back rows where the confirmation class sits importantly seem like an impossible dream.

That Bethany Evangelical Lutheran would hold its program on Christmas Eve was carved in stone. The pastor didn't care to change just to accommodate a few families that might want to travel for the holidays. In the fifties most small-town families stayed at home anyway. The sons and daughters who had left for school or jobs in "The Cities" came home to attend the service, where those who were rooted, "place-bound" we say now, could say nice things about the new urban babies they would see not often enough.

The service hadn't changed in years. Yellowing booklets – Gothic German script on the left-hand pages, English translation on the right – chronologically traced the prophecies of Christ's coming and culminated in His birth. When this text was adopted many years before, most in the congregation were only a few years, a generation at most, removed from Pomerania and could have read the left pages. By the time I was ten, almost none of the old immigrants were alive. Few younger people could read German.

The predictability of the verses and songs meant stability, an unchanging church, Luther's rock. I could speculate every fall about the passages I would be assigned. Was a hard verse a vote of confidence or a punishment?

It came out the same way – I had to do it. I awaited the dramatic moment, when the overhead lights went dark and the huge Christmas tree lit up as we began to sing "Silent Night." Rehearsals were something else. Three Saturday mornings – all morning! – spent practicing. The confirmation class escaped their regular assignments, but this pleasure was darkened by the realization that they had to carry the singing. "You must sing loudly, and well, to help out the little ones." A few male voices always cracked during "Lo How a Rose." Puberty issued no dispensations. Every year we committed the same blunders. "No! No! It's do-me-no."

"No! No! It's Pee-eece. Two syllables. Not like a toboggan going uphill." But no matter how much practice, that sled still did its thing, and one of the Swanbergs always sang "da-min-o," loudly.

The Swanbergs irritated me. They would arrive just before the service buzzing about the presents they had just opened. "I got a red dump truck," Tommy would say. "I got an electric train," Georgie would add. Charlie would gloat, "I got a panzer tank division." I never had anything to brag about. We opened our presents on Christmas morning. What good did it do to say, "I'm getting a filling station and a Farm-all tractor, but we haven't opened them up yet."? I tried that once. Charlie said, "How do you know it isn't a checker set or a flannel shirt?" Besides I wasn't getting a Sinclair station or a tractor. The Swanbergs always got nicer stuff from Santa. Why pretend?

One year a small measure of poetic justice struck them. While the ushers were distributing the treats in the classes, and while the congregation joined in the singing of "O Come All Ye Faithful," Georgie tipped over his bag while peeking in it.

Why anyone looked in these bags was a mystery to me. Every year they were the same: a grocery sack of peanuts in the shell, a few almonds and Brazil nuts, and an apple or orange. A smaller bag swelled with red, orange, and green striped hard candy and conical chocolates with insipid white centers. Looking didn't do any good. The main thing was to get in there and start eating. To crack half a dozen peanuts and put them in your mouth, insert two or three pieces of candy, and crunch up your own junk food sandwich.

Nevertheless, each year the pastor sternly warned us to stay out of the bags until services were over. In those days before Assertive Discipline he didn't have to spell out the consequences, but we still punctuated the final notes of the carol with the rustling of half-opened bags. The Swanbergs were the worst violators. They were that kind of family. So when Georgie's bag tipped over, spilling candy out into the aisle, I looked with joy at the glare in the pastor's eyes. The look on his face was my first intimation of the possibilities of the laser as a weapon of destruction.

Most congregation members didn't get upset about such breeches of protocol. They welcomed these accidents as though they were scripted into the ritual. The biggest bond between adults and children in those days was the feeling, or hope, that things would stay the same forever. Lionel Barrymore would play Scrooge on WCCO every Christmas Eve, the same families would sit in the same pews every service, the family farm would remain the backbone of the nation, and Wabasso would always be a place where people didn't have to lock their doors at night.

Even as they sat there, though, changes were coming: the Korean War was a watershed that spelled the end of many small towns as the young people left for jobs at Honeywell or wherever opportunities might arise in "The Cities." Not much longer could large families afford to live on small farms.

As children we didn't know these things yet. To us the only change was our inexorable passage one row father back each year. We were so fortunate in those quiet fifties to have time to grow up slowly without worrying about global starvation, racial prejudice, Middle East strife, energy and pollution problems, or the disintegration of the nuclear family. No, we only had to remember our verses and wonder what might be inside the brightly colored packages at home under the tree.

Chapter 38

Mr. Gadon

Shakespeare asked, "What's in a name?" That's easy to answer. If you have a name like Ernest Hemingway or Alexander the Great, you're bound to be a big success. The only exception I ever saw to this rule was Vic Hitler, the narcoleptic night club comedian on the old *Hill Street Blues*, who had trouble getting bookings because there was nothing funny about World War II.

If you can't have a famous name, have one that is easy for others to pronounce, American names like Peterson or Smith. Not one American President has had a name that any third grader could not read. On the other hand, I always run into problems when I tell people my name.

The college professor who prides himself on his ability to sight read names – after all his field is linguistics – tells the graduate seminar, "Since this is a small class, we want to get to know each other by name. If I mispronounce your name, let me know right away." When corrected, his only response is a narrowing of his eye and crisply drawn "C" in his mental gradebook. But what can you expect of a man whose PH.D. thesis titled "Communication Failures of East Saxon as Revealed Through Analysis Using Transformational Grammar as a Linguistic Model?"

High tech doesn't like my name either. I do all my thinking in front of a Smith Corona Spell-Right Dictionary Memory Typewriter. It beeps every time I try to spell a word the way it makes sense, like "nite." Or my name.

Then there are the telephone solicitors. No one can exude more confidence while mispronouncing a name as they attempt to sell you a twenty-volume set of *Pets of America*. They say, "Mr. Gadon, is there any reason why you could not pay $12 a month for a set of books that will change your life?"

When I worked at the canning factory in Cokato, I got perverse enjoyment from telling people I lived in Annandale. I always knew what would happen next.

"Oh, you're from Annandale. What's your name, then?"

Upon hearing it, their eyes would glaze over, the head would shake slightly from side to side, and the mental dial turned back to peaceful, rural Annandale of 1949, a place where strangers visited but didn't stay, a place where people listened to the Weavers sing "Good Night Irene" over WCCO.

Sometimes they would go on to ask, "Oh, you must be a newcomer?"

"Yes," I would reply, "we moved to Annandale in 1971."

Once I tried using a simple alias, Don Gordon, to avoid confusing people, but I had to quit when they started asking me who I was related to. Even a simple lie fails to win out over people who know the family trees of everyone in town.

One bizarre note to add about these conversations. The other seldom tells me his or her name. After all, they know who they are.

It's strange how people will form instant impressions based on names. Certain names are magic in a town, and the reputation of the name spreads throughout half the county like the circles that form when somebody throws a stone in a pond. "Oh, are you Linus Hillesheim's boy?" On the other hand, lack of one of these elite names handicaps a person for life.

A good example of this kind of small-town chauvinism occurred at a football game between Farmington High School, where I was then teaching, and neighboring New Prague. As I looked over the Czech names on the program, I heard a familiar voice saying, "They sure have funny names in that town." Turning around, I saw that the speaker, sure enough, was junior class *bon vivant* Jerry Ziebenfuss.

One way to broaden our thinking is to look for names that are common in some cities but rare or unknown in our own city. Looking into my collection of phone books, I find listed in one city dozens of Bambeneks, Cichanowskis, Drazkowskis, and Przyblskies, while prevalent names in another city include Benson, Hanson, and Ellefson. Any of these names would have been unusual in my hometown which teemed with Hammerschmidts, Guetters, Altermatts, and Holtznagels, a town in which anyone without a German name answered to the nickname "Swede." In that town of 600 people, there were three "Swedes," including "Swede" La Vasseur.

Maybe provincialism about names is good, though. It keeps people in their hometown, it keeps them from going far away to college, and it keeps them from the deteriorating effects of new ideas. While Robert Frost said, "Home is where they have to unlock the door," or something like that, maybe what he really meant is "Home is where they recognize your name."

One time I get real pleasure from having an uncommon name is when those letters that promise to trace your genealogy come in the mail: "There are 12 households in the U.S. with the surname Gadow." When I read that, I feel like one of the few surviving members of an endangered species, dinosaurs who migrated from the family estate in Pomerania sometime in the 1800s, after serfdom was abolished, and fell victim to the Buffalo guns of those with common names.

By the way, you people with common names, how many relatives do you have listed Webster's Biographical Dictionary?

- Gadow (ga'do) Hans Friedrich. 1855-1928. Zoologist, b. Pomerania; curator and lecturer on morphology of vertebrates, Cambridge U., England (from 1884). Author of *A Classification of Vertebrata* (1898), *The Wandering of Animals*, etc.

Like great great uncle Hans Friedrich, the etc. says a lot about me too.

Chapter 39
Soap opera update

To fulfill the many, many requests, here is a soap opera update for the people who are too busy to view their favorite show because they have to work.

Municipal Liquor Store. Jake removed "Jailhouse Rock" from the jukebox. Angered, the town council votes 3-2 against free popcorn during happy hour. Upset when *Cheers* is pre-empted for a Barbara Walters special interview of Bo Gritz, Seth throws a barstool through the TV set. Jake catches Verlyn stealing a case of liquor. Wendy is fired for cashing too many bad checks.

Main Street Blues. Eighteen-inch snowfall causes crisis in the snow removal budget. Big run on gas line antifreeze and starting fluid at Circle D Farm Store. Sheriff closes Simson's Bordello. Coffee crowd supports Bush's statement on hunger in America, knocks the Timberwolves. Verlyn's uncle Erle wants Jake fired. Chamber of Commerce wants the World Trade Center moved here to stimulate town growth and keep the hotels filled. Clover Supermarket features rutabagas on special.

Back Forty. Axel is snuffed out. Poachers steal twelve of Ralph's traps. After eating traditional fish head soup every Saturday night for eighteen years, Tumo finally tells Rachel that he hates any food that looks back at him. Shep cleans out the chicken house. Emil subscribes to *Finns and Feathers*. Axel returns from town with a full roll of Copenhagen, vowing never to run out "agan." Axel shoots Shep. Aunt Ondine decides to keep her baby.

One life to Lib. When Dexter holds the door open for Zona, she slams it in his face. Trink files sexual harassment suit against Mr. Clark. Reeba looks for a surrogate father for the child she wishes to have. Aggie buys little

Mandy a toy hard hat. Sharlyn Borshtnikov and Grant Jonchowski decide to honor each other in marriage by taking each other's names. Instead of Sharlyn Borshtnikov-Jonchowski and Grant Borshtnikov-Jonchowski, Max suggests they use, "Mr. And Mrs. Bo Jo Jones." The Organization Versus All Men (OVAM) asks the school board to remove all library books showing pictures of housewives or men driving road construction equipment.

At the Ritz. The Continental doesn't start during cold weather. Travis waits nine hours for emergency road service. Felix eats ten dollars worth of caviar when Joshua accidentally leaves the refrigerator door open. Karl discusses tax loopholes with his tax accountant, who has just been unjustly incarcerated in federal prison at Sandstone. Since they already have everything one could want, Travis and Jinx decide to give each other creative Christmas presents – a glad hand, a telescope for taking a look at things, a flashlight for shedding light on the subject, a set of pseudo values, a shinola detector, a wagon load of grist for the rumor mill, lounging furniture for their long-standing beliefs, boots and a walking staff to help daughter Jill with next year's college tuition hikes.

Big Shed Country. Jerome changes the Blazer's oil and filter. Chad's snowmobile blows its track, setting off the old family argument about personal responsibility. Melva bakes a cake from scratch, but Jerome thinks she used a box mix. With snow too deep for four-wheeling, Jerome rides nine miles to town by snowmobile to buy a case of beer and cash his workman's comp check that he gets for his back injury. Seeing Jerome leave, Derrick visits Melva and eats cake. Likes it. Mack spears a 19-pound northern. Nora tells him he can't hang it in the living room if he gets it mounted. The six Finleys show family togetherness by going to town to mail their unemployment claims simultaneously.

Paw and Mawd. Paw is having his old problem again. Mawd's shoelace factory is found in violation of 37 OSHA regulations. Mawd vows to shut down before giving in to those "snooty snoops from Liar City." Jeffroe is kidnapped and held for ransom. Paw tries in vain to convince Mawd to pay the money to get her dad back. The town is evacuated when a railroad tanker containing sulphuric acid is derailed. Paw sneaks back into town because the smell reminds him of lutefisk. Clyde wins the cribbage tournament at the Legion Club. Winston falls into the lace tip press, sparking an investigation by Sparky Duveiller, Mawd's chief flunky, of worker carelessness.

Tamarack Literary Society. Professor William F. X. Henswar, of Panatella State University, speaks to the entire society on "Literary Qualities of

Harlequin Romances," receives a standing ovation. The genealogy group during the past week has discovered the following famous ancestors and present relatives: pirates Black Beard, Blue Beard, Red Beard, and Double Pinochle; Martin Luther; Alex Haley; sixteenth century statesman Left Bower; Princess Grace of Monaco; Brigham Young; Philip the restless, eighteenth century German playboy; Judge Crater; horse thief Stretch Connors; and singer Tiny Tim. Philo reviews *The Simpsons*. Several members drop out of the genealogist section after reading Sinclair Lewis's novel *Kingsblood Royal*. Feena vows to finish the *Unfinished Symphony*, Professor Twilogy finds the *Lost Chord*. The Long Lake Pig Farm and Counterculture Life Style and Electronic Game Commune begins publishing their own newspaper *The Agitate*. Census by society members at the last flea market of the season reveals a total of 10,789 books for sale that day, dominated by 1263 Harlequins, 3692 swashbucklers, and 237 copies of *Once is Not Enough*. Hiram suggests bird watching for next year's census, but he is hooted down. As Miss Bunner remarks, "Birds are for shooting, not looking at.

"

Chapter 40

Indian summer

Sitting in the front seat of my 1963 Mercury Comet convertible, I reached around my wife. "Ouch," she exclaimed, as the ice and cold pop spilled down the front of her sweater. "If you have to make a mess all over me, at least do it with your popcorn. It's not so cold." Because I had only two hands to hold my snacks with, I gave up on the romance and settled back to watch *Revenge of the Nerds* on the drive-in theater screen. The drama unfolded while I mediated on the long road that had brought me to this milestone in my life.

The last part of that long road had stretched that evening from Annandale to Little Falls, which had the closest A&W Drive-in. Then it led back to St. Cloud to the outdoor movie, the passion pit, the teenage Las Vegas. The beginnings of that road stretched back to 1956, when I first lusted after a new Ford convertible. I was broke, but the dream died hard. When the retractable hard top came out a couple of years later, I determined to get one. My bank account was short only $5,624, but I knew that every dog must have its day.

The dream was revived in the early 80s , when my life entered into neo-adolescence, or what a highly-placed executive of a liquor joint called "male menopause." That's the stage of life when 40-year-olds wear white shoes and spend lots of time staring at the back ends of tight jeans. I decided that my life had to be more than wearing a "45 and Holding" T-shirt. I would do my own thing, whatever that thing might be.

I stared at the velvet painting of Elvis in the living room. It came to me – the car makes the man. I needed a car that would express my personality. The little woman responded, "That dirty, rusted out 1970 Ford out there, the one with the bad valve, says it all."

"No," I answered, chuckling at her feeble joke. "I mean the inner self. The latent side of me, that hidden potential. My esthetic sense."

"Can you take out the garbage? That leftover cabbage smells."

I went to an auto show and picked out my convertible. As the seller and I exchanged keys for cash, I mentioned in farewell, "People always stare at me anyway. I might as well give them a real eyeful. And the wife gets to go topless now."

"I'm gonna do the same thing," he said. "I got a chance to buy a 1959 Ford retractable hard top, fire engine red."

There's only one thing wrong with driving a convertible in Minnesota – cool and rainy summers. Regardless, when I got home, I put the top down, then went in the house to put on my parka and sorrel boots. Nothing would stop me, I said to myself, from showing off this car, nothing except rain. As I stepped out the door, pellets of rain bounced off my glasses. I ran to the car and put up the top. It can't rain every day, I rationalized.

A family conference hammered out a few rules about the car's use. "We'll take it out once to each place we usually go to so we can brag about it. Then we'll hold down the miles. Let's make it last another 22 years. Oh, and we don't take it to the Kimball dance hall. And no driving on roads under construction."

"That takes care of most driving," one of the kids said.

"I have a rule of my own," added my wife. "Nobody, repeat nobody, will drive it wearing bib overalls." I went to the bedroom to change clothes.

We took it to the South Haven fish fry, to a housewarming, to show off to various friends. Then I headed to one of my favorite night spots, the South Haven liquor store.

I nodded to a few casual acquaintances near the bar. Then I spotted a familiar bald pot. Raising the head off the bar, I said, "Jackie, come outside and see my new car. It's a (pause for voice deepening ala Ted Baxter delivering the WJM news) CONVERTIBLE." His head slumped back on the bar top. "Come on. You don't see a car like this every day."

"It's about time somebody got this guy our of here," the bartender said. "He's your baby." I wrestled his car keys away from him.

Jackie stared at the car a few seconds. He turned his bloodshot eyes toward me and slurred, "You ought to jack it up and put a four wheel drive train in it. It'd be a heckofa ice fishing car. You could fish right over the side, like fishing out of a boat but no waves."

"See you around, Jackie," I said. "Stay between the ditches."

"Naw, I'm walking home. There's too many drunks on the road."

On Sunday I puttered around the yard all day, never straying far from the convertible. A few people drove slowly past and stared, but nobody stopped. About four in the afternoon a neighbor came over, big smile on his face. "Have you seen my garbage can lid? A green one? It blew away last week that windy day."

"No," I answered, flicking the chamois over the car's blue paint.

"Well, I gotta keep looking. Say, that Viking game was a real bummer, huh?"

The movie was ending. All the Nerds of the world could rejoice. It was a moral victory for all the poor souls who wear black horn-rimmed glasses. I started up the car and pushed in my surfing tape.

"Say, put up the top. It's freezing in here."

I hated to admit it, but I had been cold all through the movie. "I'm cold too. It feels like December."

I ran the top up, turned off the tape, and switched on WCCO. I never liked Jan and Dean anyway.

Chapter 41
The legend of the boxelder bug

By early spring we're harassed by the first box elder bug of the season as the warm weather brings them out to play hide and seek in our houses. Remember that crawling feeling on the back of the neck? The feeling of joy as you pluck it off and crush it under your heel? The agonizing reality that you can never kill them all? That no matter what you do they will always get into your house?

These bugs rank low in nature's hierarchy, lower than deer flies, gnats, starlings, and eelpout. The only use I ever found for them was as a tool to victimize little girls at school. By the time I was 16 or 17, the novelty had worn off.

The box elder tree itself is not desirable. Although it grows rapidly, its value as a shade tree is diminished by its poor shape, weak branches and trunk that splits easily. As firewood it ranks somewhere between poplar and 2x4 scraps.

Although the Midwest is filled with box elder trees now, according to my *Encyclopedia of General Knowledge and Useful Facts*, this member of the maple family was once confined in small numbers to a single grove of trees in central Ohio. The story of how this tree spread is an interesting American legend.

As a young man in the Buckeye State, Hieronymous Baches was converted during the Second Great Awakening into a small religious sect which believed that the new inventions and economic and philosophical forces that were altering the traditional values of this country were being spread by the devil, who was rapidly gaining the upper hand in this world. After being ordained an Elder in this sect, Baches became obsessed by the personal vision that he must reform the Midwest. At the same time he felt tremendous frustration over the scope of this task, a labor that he felt personally inadequate to carry out.

Then one night inspiration came to him while he was coon hunting. During his boyhood he had come to hate a particular variety of tree found in a huge woods surrounding his farm home. This tree was referred to by the unlettered members of the Baches family as "bug tree" because it sent out tens of millions of little red and black bugs to forage in neighboring houses and cow barns. Hieronymous decided to travel the northern half of the continent selling seedlings of this tree. Once planted, these trees would inflict the entire population of this area with bugs so obnoxious that they would counteract the vices of gluttony, greed, and sensuality with doses of the corresponding virtues of humility, patience, and self-sacrifice.

That fall Baches purchased a team of horses and a wagon, dug 5,000 dormant saplings, wrapped their roots, and set off from home to sell, give away, or plant these trees under the dark of the moon. Representing them as sugar maples, Baches sold out quickly.

As Baches left for home, this alter-ego of Johnny Appleseed felt little pleasure from his accomplishment. Although his knowledge of geography was limited to a third-grade education in his local little red school house, he knew he had a long way to go before he would cover all the Midwest with his "bug trees."

The next spring he dug 10,000 seedlings and hired a boy to drive a second wagon. By November the pair had penetrated into Indiana. Still, the fear that he would die before he accomplished his task nagged at Baches continually. After all, he was 22 already.

Then new inspiration came to him. He would gather the seeds of the trees and distribute them from one wagon, while he sold seedlings from the other. That fall when he set out with his young companion Cotton Mather Buckholtz, he had enough seeds alone to plant 500,000 trees.

As a conscientious objector during the Civil War, Baches' progress was not slowed by military service. He trekked endlessly over the plains, reaching Illinois in 1863, Wisconsin in 1869, Iowa in 1874, and finally Minnesota in 1878.

By this time his reputation had preceded him. Settlers of the treeless Sea of Grass eagerly awaited his arrival. Immigrants scarcely off the boat at Ellis Island heard about these trees that would provide shade and maple syrup.

In their broken English they told each other how much they wanted to get some of "dem" trees of Baches Elders. In 1891 a dictionary standardized the name and spelling as we refer to it today, box elder.

As Baches lay dying in 1889, his last thoughts were bittersweet. The pleasure of knowing how much moral reform he had sown throughout the Midwest was mingled with disappointment at covering only seven states. Knowing that the sap of these trees could be boiled down to produce a tasty syrup – thus he had spread pleasure along with religious suffering – bothered him also. Fortunately for his spiritual movement few people ever came to know about the syrup or tried a second time to make it.

He died near DeSmet, South Dakota, while trying to figure out how to spread grasshopper and locust infestations to prevent backsliding by the new generation of pioneers, who preferred cottonwood trees.

By spreading the bugs, however, Baches left us a lasting legacy, while accomplishing his role of missionary and prophet. Relaxing under a shade tree would never be the same in the Midwest.

Today there is only one way to get rid of box elder disease: cut down the tree, burn all the wood and branches, chip the stump, and carry away all the litter. After two or three years the bugs should have disappeared. Unless, that is, your neighbor has his own box elder tree.

Chapter 42

The wily green fly

We called him Ishmael, an outcast and wanderer. Like the narrator of *Moby Dick*, he felt the damp, drizzly weather deep down in his soul; but instead of going to sea like Melville's hero, our Ishmael decided to ride out the winter warm and dry and safe in our house.

At first we admired him for his Coke-bottle green coloring and his gigantic size – as big as a teenage girl's thumbnail. He seemed the perfect representation of the species Diptera, or superfly. He (we gave him an Olympic-type sex test to avoid any chauvinistic treatment) spent most of those early October days basking in the light that shone through the windows onto the cat's food dishes. Heeding the warning of Coleridge and James Herriot:

"He prayeth best, who loveth best

All things both great and small."

we let the great green fly live in peace.

Even the cat seemed to like Ishmael. The cat and the fly never interfered with each other's positions at the food dishes. Through the weeks their relationship evolved from coexistence to genuine affection.

Things changed one day when one of my more iconoclastic neighbors dropped in for a visit. "Wow! Look at that huge fly! It looks like a lead actor from a Nippon Studios mutation film." I feigned nonchalance. "Oh yeah. I'd better get the fly swatter."

The swatter, a Christmas gift from a local store, was a blue one. Its color must have touched off vibrations along Ishmael's DEW line. As I took it off the wall, he rose from the cat dish, bits of Tender Vittles dropping from his body as his huge wings carried him away to parts unknown.

"Ya gotta move faster. Ya didn't even get a shot at the sucker," the neighbor complained. Inwardly I was relieved.

Ishmael vanished until the next afternoon. Just as I was settling down for my daily nap, I heard the familiar buzzing noise, like a chainsaw with a dull blade bogging down in a white oak log. Whether he was motivated by anger and revenge or by a desire to forgive what he sensed as a betrayal on my part, I don't know. Maybe, like a neighbor, he just wanted to borrow my lawn mower. Whatever his motives, he buzzed around for fifteen minutes. Finally I got up, unrested but gladdened to see that Ishmael was undaunted.

From that time on I saw Ishmael only once a day at nap time. A little ritual developed; I would hear his buzzing, I would put a pillow over my head and draw the covers over my face, Ishmael would somehow get under the covers and buzz gleefully, I would get up unrefreshed, forced once again to do something constructive. He had become a Dipteraic defender of the work ethic.

One day when I was especially tired, I snapped and vowed to get Ishmael. Unfortunately, the fly swatter had disappeared. (It turned up about six weeks later among a pile of newspapers and magazines that I intended to look at some day.)

As Ishmael buzzed in blissful ignorance, little did he know that he would soon be blotting out half of Reggie Jackson's face. The rolled-up *Sporting News* with Mr. October on the cover was ready. After all, that much money for a .218 hitter!

Those who have tried to swat a fly with a rolled-up newspaper or other such ersatz device know what happened next. Those who have never attempted this futility would not believe any explanation. Oh, he was a wily one!

Day after day I went napless. I turned into a reincarnation of Captain Ahab, relentlessly pursuing the great green fly. One day I almost got him with a Newsweek profile of Yassar Arafat, but as Confucius once said, "Close counts in horseshoes."

Then one day I remembered Giraudoux's short play, *The Apollo of Bellac*, in which a young girl is told that the secret of life is flattery. To learn the art of telling men that they are handsome, she practices on a fly. I resolved to try the same tactics. After all, folk wisdom tells us that we catch more flies with honey than with manure. I settled down at naptime, folded the St. Cloud *Times* at my side, waiting for Ishmael.

He soon started on his first cord of wood for the afternoon. "How handsome you are," I intoned. He buzzed around. "What a nice green color you are." He buzzed closer. "What a big proboscis, what handsome labella." Still closer. "Your goatee-like antennae make you look very intellectual." Almost there. "You obviously aren't from Iowa." He settled down on the bedspread. Zap! Carefully I raise the newspaper and looked at the editorial page. Kilpatrick's column was still all right. Ishmael had escaped again.

The next day I set out a plate of manure. All that accomplished was getting the bedspread tracked up. Ishmael had won. No more naps. Then I remembered that I had not mailed out the required twenty copies of the good luck chain letter I had received about a week before. "Don't send money, as fate has no price," the letter stated. "Dolan Fairchild received the letter and, not believing, threw the letter away. Nine days later he died." I feverishly began addressing envelopes to people who seemed to need good luck: Steve Dils, Calvin Griffith, Roberto Duran, Liz Taylor, Ted Kennedy, Tattoo.

I made several trips through the house carrying the stack of envelopes and calling out "No mas." If Ishmael spotted my good intentions he didn't let on. I felt like O. Henry's heroine in "The Last Leaf." Ishmael was the last fly of fall. Maybe I would be doomed if something happened to him. Or was there still time for the chain letter to save me?

Somewhere in this story can be found answers to such questions as "Why respect nature?" "What does flattery accomplish?" "Why did the House Un-American Activities Committee once investigate relaxation?" and, most important of all, "How powerful is a good luck chain letter?" Ishmael returned, and I was healed. Chain letters work. The cat was happy too.

Chapter 43
Big shedders

I first used my signature term, "Big Shed Country," to define Central Minnesota, an area that twenty years ago was dotted with 12x60 mobile homes alongside 30x40 steel pole buildings. The old man was out in the shed carving up a Chevy with a cutting torch while the Ms. was in the trailer trying to simultaneously wrap clean diapers around three kids.

The trailer was a temporary stage, a starter home, but when they built their dream house, a five bedroom three level with a handful of bathrooms, there was room on the ten acres for another big shed. It became clear to me that being a Big Shedder is not a socio-economic condition but an attitude. It also became clear that all of us Midwesterners are Shedders at heart, at least we men are.

Big Shedders once got a thrill out of Lawrence Welk's bubble machine. Now we're in love with Ross Perot's smoke machine. We hate politics until we need our road graded. We support education until it's time to pay our taxes.

We paint our CB handle on the pickup stone deflector, but we won't paint our name on our mailbox. We dress up these pickups with an array of running lights, glow-in-the-dark running boards, and enough flame to reenact the Great Chicago Fire. We'll put on the dog but not a necktie. Our mating call is the rumble of gigantic tires.

Because we believe in physical fitness, we'll jog five miles. That's before we cut a postage stamp lawn with a riding mower and sit in a golf cart for eighteen holes.

We fear death but go deer hunting.

Our sense of humor is a step above sophomoric. It's junioric.

We do our reading in the most comfortable, poorest lit, and least ambient room in the house.

We drive five miles to see if our friend wants to go fishing because we hate to talk on the phone, but we listen for ten minutes to a sales rep's cold call because we don't know how to hang up the phone.

Harmon Killebrew was a bum because he didn't hit a grand slam the day we drove to the Met from Swanville.

We complain about the wife's cooking but go out to eat tasteless, dry fast-food hamburgers on stale buns. In a typical night at the bar we eat a turkey gizzard, two pickled eggs, three bags of chips, and a partridge in a pear tree. Plus enough popcorn to float a battleship. Then we wash it down with light beer.

We hate big cities, but we'll hang out with thousands at the Mall of America. We brag about buying our clothes at Dayton's but don't mention they're channeled through Target.

We drive 55 Alive on the highway and 45 in town. We sit for fifteen minutes in the Dairy Queen drive-through instead of walking up and getting instance service. We're always in a hurry and getting nowhere. We get right up close to the car in front of us so we can read the bumper stickers.

We drive in the ten and two position, unless we think it's noon or 6:30. Trained jugglers, we can drive with a cigarette in one hand, a coffee cup in the other, while reading a road map. No, that's wrong. We don't use maps.

Like loyal foot soldiers, we hurry up and wait. We get to church early so we can grab the rear pews so we can get right out when it's over.

We believe in family values, then watch *Married with Children*.

Rugged individualists, we won't curry favors with the boss, but we'll network with him/her.

Most of these examples describe men. To round the picture, I asked my wife to mention a few paradoxical behaviors of women. She said, "There aren't any."

"You mean women are perfect, or close to it?" I asked.

"Close."

Chapter 44

Ashes to ashes, rust to dust

As the song says, there's a time to fold 'em in, and that's true for cars as well as cards. "Never throw away what you can fix," the old timers say. Well, that idea has gone the way of the Stanley Steamer. By the time my 1970 Ford headed for its final resting place, it was costing me a 20 here, a 30 there, a 75 dollar bill every month.

Heavy cars like that are good demolition derby material. I tried to sell it to a neighbor who lives dangerously. "Just listen to that engine purr," I said, as I ground the starter. "Hang on, it'll fire any minute." I ground some more, but it wouldn't turn over. I removed the air cleaner and stuck a big screwdriver in the choke. "Works every time." The engine engaged with a vibration that would match any electric plant dynamo.

"Sounds like a good deal," said the neighbor. "I'm in a race, the car stalls, I crawl out the window with my big screwdriver, unchain the hood, open the choke, and some guy in a big station wagon cuts my legs off." He walked home.

Summer is the wrong time to sell a mobile ice fishing house. It was time to drive it to the French Lake Auto Parts, better known as the French Lake junk yard, or Junktown, USA. That's where my car would be appreciated for what it's worth – a couple of wheels, some copper, and a lot of scrap iron.

My head filled with memories as I drove the green monster for the last time. Disappointment at the car's failure by a trip to Kimball and back to make the longed for 100,000 miles. Pleasure from the recollection of the many fish that had been caught through the holes in the floor boards.

Oldest son Eric had used the car for college transportation for several years. Instead of studying calculus in it, though, he used it mostly as a fishing car, hauling him to Red Lake, Lindsey Lake, and that remote walk-in, carry-in lake known to natives of the Bemidji area as No Name Lake.

The last few years I had used it mostly for short trips-to the post office, the bank, the baseball diamond – but I wouldn't have been afraid to drive it to Maple Lake or Buffalo if necessary. Now with its insurance and license ready to expire, it had been cut from our roster of cars by the wife's big Buick.

"It's your lucky day," I told the fellows at the junk yard. They chuckled politely but weren't impressed. "Sounds tired," Floyd said after listening to the engine. "Well, it's like me," I said. "Been on a lot of gravel roads, climbed a lot of mountains, watched too much television instead of exercising or weeding the garden."

Back inside I turned over the title. "Looks like you're signing the death certificate," a spectator remarked. The joke seemed as worn out as the car. I have wondered if junk yards have their spectators, their hangers-on, who sit around watching people surrender their dreams.

"Just a minute." I had forgotten to take the big screwdriver out of the carburetor. Overcome with nostalgia I removed the old bed sheet that had been stuffed in the holes of the trunk to keep out the snow and dust. I cast a final glance at the back seat, which had torn loose from its moorings. I thought of the faulty accessory switch that had caused me a two mile walk during below zero weather because playing the radio while I was jigging a Rapala had drained the battery down even lower than the temperature.

I left with the money, a generous amount, but not enough of course. How much would yell sell a friend for? I heard the sound of air hissing, that telltale sign of bad valves that I heard every time I shut off the Ford's motor. "Psssst. Hey Bud." I kept on walking. "Psssst. You."

I turned. An elderly gentleman attired in bib overalls, Leef Brothers cap, and four day growth of whiskers was beckoning me to the side of the building. "Me?"

"Ya, you, commere."

"What do you want?"

"I heard you talking in dere about your garden. Sounds bad."

"Yes, I can't ever seem to grow a decent garden. The ground's hard as a rock. Every July the weed inspector gets after me. I go out every day and look at it, but it doesn't seem to help."

"Well, dere's a old secret to gardens. From da old country."

"What is it?"

"No, you gotta buy it. Success don't come cheap."

"How much?"

"Five dollars."

"Five dollars for a little gardening advice?"

"Dat's right, but it's not a little advice. It's da big secret. Vorks every time."

"All right. Here's your five dollars."

He handed me a sealed envelope, one of those small, cheap ones that drug stores put on sale two boxes for one dollar. "You got to vait till you get home vit it. It ripens vile you drive." He slunk around the corner.

"Wait, what if I have some questions about this method? How can I get ahold of you?"

"You von't. It's simple as junking out a car."

Well, I cheated him. I had the envelope torn open before I reached the turn off by the big transformer. On a piece of paper torn out of a seed corn notebook were these words:

"HARD VORK."

Made in the USA
Monee, IL
04 November 2023

45775513R00080